PENGUIN BOOKS

LANTERN SLIDES

Edna O'Brien was born in the west of Ireland and now lives in London. One of Britain's most gifted contemporary writers, she is the author of *The Country Girls*, *The Lonely Girl* (published in Penguin as *Girl with Green Eyes*) and *Girls in their Married Bliss*, published in one volume as *The Country Girls Trilogy*. Her other books include *August is a Wicked Month*, *Casualties of Peace*, *The Love Object*, *A Pagan Place*, *Zee and Co.*, *Mother Ireland*, *Night*, *A Scandalous Woman and Other Stories*, *Johnny I Hardly Knew You*, *Mrs Reinhardt and Other Stories*, *Returning* and *A Fanatic Heart*. All of these are published by Penguin. She has also written several plays, including *Virginia* (a life of Virginia Woolf) and *A Pagan Place*.

EDNA O'BRIEN

LANTERN SLIDES

SHORT STORIES

PENGUIN BOOKS

PENGUIN BOOKS

Published by the Penguin Group
Penguin Books Ltd, 27 Wrights Lane, London W8 5TZ, England
Viking Penguin, a division of Penguin Books USA Inc.
375 Hudson Street, New York, New York 10014, USA
Penguin Books Australia Ltd, Ringwood, Victoria, Australia
Penguin Books Canada Ltd, 2801 John Street, Markham, Ontario, Canada L3R 1B4
Penguin Books (NZ) Ltd, 182–190 Wairau Road, Auckland 10, New Zealand

Penguin Books Ltd, Registered Offices: Harmondsworth, Middlesex, England

First published by George Weidenfeld & Nicolson 1990
Published in Penguin Books 1991
1 3 5 7 9 10 8 6 4 2

Some of these stories were first published, in somewhat different form in the *New Yorker*, *Paris Review* and *Antaeus*.

Printed in England by Clays Ltd, St Ives plc

To Antoinette

'Each human life must work through all the joys and sorrows, gains and losses, which make up the history of the world.'

Thomas Mann

Contents

'OFT IN THE STILLY NIGHT'

IT IS A SMALL SOMNOLENT VILLAGE with a limestone rock that sprawls irregularly over the village green, where sprouts a huge beech tree along with incidental saplings that meander out of it. Picturesque, you might say. Life has a quiet hum to it. You are passing through, on your way to somewhere livelier. You would never dream that so many restless souls reside here, dreaming of a different destiny. As you enter you see a stone, Roman-type church, one of the oldest in the land, a graveyard adjoining it and, on the tombstones, huge white lozenges of lichen that look bold, if not to say comic. In contrast a ball alley next door is green and oozes damp from years of rain. This is a rainy hamlet, being on the Gulf Stream. You would rarely come across anyone playing handball, except perhaps on Sundays, when a few youths, having trampled over grave plots and flower domes, take it into their heads to give themselves another bit of diversion by pegging a ball or some stones at the green lamenting cement. However, they soon tire of that and move on to amuse themselves with old cars or old motorcycles.

The effect when you first enter is of a backwater where souls and bodies have fallen prey to a stubborn tedium.

You will find dogs, many of them mongrels, chasing each other over the ample green or snoozing in the sun. In the grocery shop the prevailing smell will be of flour and grain stuff and if you are lucky you might find bananas or grapes but most likely you will have to settle for apples. You could be tempted by a wide open-faced biscuit, like the face of a clock, studded with dark brown raisins. You would not suspect that in the big house with the wrought-iron gateway and the winding overgrown avenue a wife went a little peculiar, lost her marbles. It is said that it was her sister's fault, her sister, Angela. After spending many years in a convent, Angela to the chagrin of her order and her relatives upped and left, and came to live with Margaret in the big house. At first she hid, even from Margaret's husband, but gradually when her hair grew she emerged from her bedroom and eventually ventured down to the drawing room, to give a tinkle on the piano. It is said that it was there the husband, Ambrose, first saw her in a secular outfit, because of course he had seen her as a nun. Ambrose, who was something of a fop, was immediately captivated by her beauty and the slenderness of her frame inside a long brown velvet dress that buttoned down the centre and had a flare. Anything can happen to three people who languish in a house, a big house, a damp house, a house with gongs on the kitchen wall and many dank passages which could do with a lick of paint but for a chronic shortage of money. People can drive each other mad in such circumstances. Angela ate like a bird, gardened and played the piano in the evenings. Also she sang. She sang 'Oft In The Stilly Night' and 'There's A Bridle Hanging On The Wall'. In the summer evenings, with the bow window open, her voice could be heard by children or people milking in the fields nearby and it was thought to be rather screeching. The gardener who went there once a week to do a bit of scything stole their gooseberries and refused to oil the hinges of the lych-gate or do any extra favours because they never invited him indoors or offered him a cup of tea, being too stuck-up. Neighbours said he had every right to take the gooseberries and plagued him for a little can for themselves. They were very sweet gooseberries, yellow, translucent.

The sisters, Angela and Margaret, quarrelled a lot; at times so bitterly that Angela's belongings were flung out the window – dresses, a corset, her prayer book and beads, and the fur tippet which she wore at Mass and which sported the narrow and knowing face of a little fox. Ambrose, however, always intervened and Angela was dragged back from the avenue or even beyond the gate if she had ventured so far. No one knew or could imagine how peace was restored, what strategies of sweetness or authority Ambrose had had to resort to. What was rumoured was that he and Angela cuddled in the kitchen garden. Many people had seen them or had boasted about seeing them, and many wondered why his wife did not throw him out, since it was she who owned the house. Ambrose was something of a gentleman and shunned work. Soon as he married Margaret – the plainer sister – he rented out the land for grazing and spent his time on more dilatory pursuits, such as keeping bees and making elderflower wine. Ambrose knew so little about country matters that he was the butt of a standing joke. He had a sick beast which was too feeble to stir from its manger. He called on some locals, hoping to save himself the expense of a veterinary surgeon, and they simply turned the beast around to see if a bit of exercise might help. Ambrose, re-entering the manger after a suitable interval, said to the two men, 'Her eyes are brighter,' whereas in fact he was contemplating her rear. The two men drank liberally on the joke and, as time went by, embellished it.

Not long after Angela came to live there, tales of the

unhappy trio began to trickle out and speculation was rife indeed, some locals even promising to steal over the high wall into the kitchen garden to get a gawk through the drawing room window. No one ever visited there, because Margaret was fiendishly thrifty and often returned to the shop with a package of bacon, to say there was one rasher short. Luck was not on their side. Angela grew ill, got thinner, was obliged to see a specialist and learned that she was struck down with a wasting disease. Sympathies changed quite drastically, and her good points – her singing, her devoutness at Mass and her taste in dressing – were now promulgated. She died in June and had a quite presentable funeral. Her brother-in-law followed her before a month was out and this, of course, substantiated the clandestine love story. Margaret became an object of pity, received gifts of jam and shortbread and was invited to card games which she did not attend. Margaret herself was an invalid a few years later, crippled with rheumatoid arthritis. At first she could move about with a stick and in the post office many were eager to discuss the pain with her and to suggest cures, all of which were useless. Eventually she was house-bound.

The jubilee nurse called once a week and let herself in by the back kitchen door, which was on the latch. It was she who reported that Margaret had repaired to the bridal room, where a dormant love for her husband burgeoned and was reaching fantastic proportions. His name was constantly on her lips, stories about their courtship, the food he liked and the idealization of her until the day of his death. Local women also called but Margaret could not hear the knocker, which was rusty, and so she remained banished in that bridal room with the baize-covered shutters, unable to admit the visitors that she longed for, muttering prayers, saying her husband's name and at times getting confused in the day of the week, wondering if the jubilee nurse was due or not.

You would not know, either, that in the main street, in the row of imitation Georgian houses, many fracas lurk. There is an unfortunate woman who scrubs and cleans for a living while her husband skulks in woods to assault girls and women. Some he does not have to assault, some wanton ones it is said go there, dally and allow themselves to be hauled into thickets or bracken or verdure. A kindly girl, Oonagh, takes in washing, starches sheets and tablecloths to such a stiffness that they are like boards. Her clothes-line is never free of sheets, tablecloths, serviettes and even more private garments. Nearby a lady who has the audacity to keep tinkers actually admits them into her house and allows them up to her bedrooms, five or six to a room. Her hallway smells foul, and no wonder. Many a Monday morning she is shaking bedspreads and eiderdowns from a top window and neighbours shout caustic things, not directly to her, but to each other so that she can hear. The Flea Hotel is the nickname of her crumbling premises.

A respectable lady who lives in the cut stone house with the bow window was the victim of one of those tinkers, who stole her shoes. They were tan brogue shoes which she had decided to dye brown. While they were drying, a hussy had come begging but was not received despite incessant knocking and pleading about the babe in her arms. In pique she helped herself to the shoes.

She was caught not long after, found by the sergeant at some sort of regatta where she was telling fortunes, squatting down on a bit of red velvet, giving the impression of an Eastern sage and wearing the shoes. In the court, her accuser, a married woman dressed in a black coat with Persian lamb trimming down the front, lost her heart for retribution, remembered somehow her own childhood, her dire poverty, her ancestors having been evicted from the fertile plains and having to flee to a mountain abode, repented having reported the thing at all and asked the judge in tearful tones to overlook it and to exercise clemency. The judge, who did not like this sort of interruption on a busy day – there was an anteroom full of people with cases waiting to be heard – asked her tetchily to be a little more circumspect in the future about clemency and to save her contrition for the confessional. As the shoes were handed over, the married woman begged that the tinker woman be let keep them, but of course such a request was impossible and she left the court carrying them in her hand limply, as if she would drop them the moment she got outside. The tinker woman was given a sentence of seven days and nights in the county gaol, which could be reprieved if she paid a fine of fifty pounds. This of course was impossible and sent all the tinkers on a wild binge around the town, cursing and vowing ructions.

In another house a nervous priest who has been defrocked sits most of the day. The scandal is so great it can hardly be mentioned. His nerves are cited as the reason, but one who has travelled far has come back with a murky secret, in short, claiming that the priest had an eye for the ladies. Anyhow, he cannot say Mass, does not even serve at High Masses, and is seen on the hospital roads on Sundays walking with his mother. They gather branches to decorate their living room. They are the only people who call it by that name, as all others say parlour or drawing room and they are the only people who put flowers and branches indoors. One small clemency meted to the young priest is that insanity runs in the family since a cousin hanged himself from a tree, years back.

Yes, you would pass houses where there are drunks, where husbands on the day they get their pay packets do not come home till well after midnight, their wives accosting them on the top of the stairs or at the bottom of the stairs or wherever; and there are houses with bachelors whose rooms have never had a woman's hand to them and hence are dusty and somewhat inhospitable. You will pass various families with young children and another family which keeps horses and ponies and has had the misfortune to have one of its horses bolt out into the main road and be killed by a motorist, who then set out to sue the family for negligence.

'Spliced her in half,' the young son of the family is fond of saying, as a pathetic re-enactment of the restless mare and her mad bolting is described again and again.

You will find a former music teacher who no longer takes pupils but still keeps the sheet music on her piano to prove her former prowess, and who allows her little bantam hens the run of her house. Not far away, you will find a gentleman who was for a time like any common convict in Australia doing penal servitude, but has now returned to his roots. His crime was that he fired a shot at a barmaid who refused to serve him a drink after hours, and unfortunately he was a good shot and killed her. He no longer drinks but lives in semi-solitude, playing patience in the evening. There is a doting couple too, because of course every village has a doting couple. These are a childless pair who make their own butterscotch and resort to the most extreme endearments at all hours, even at breakfast-time. When the husband goes to work in the forestry his wife stealthily follows soon after on her bicycle, stationing herself behind the high limestone wall at the edge of the forest to make sure that her husband does not talk or mingle with any of these passing young girls or women.

There is too, in the house with the gorgeous geraniums on the porch, a budding beauty, plump, not too plump, eyes navy and limpid, eye sockets like inkwells in which this enticing navy stuff swills about, eyes ready for love. She reads magazines and cuts out the tips about hair and beauty and figure and so forth. There are children galore, housed in the school most of the time and utter nuisances during holiday time. There is a saddler's from whose doorway the pleasant smell of new leather and linseed oil drifts out, and not far away a shoemaker with the more fetid smell of sweat and old leather. That place is a jumble of old shoes heaped in an immemorial pyre. Then three mornings a week there is the heartening smell of fresh bread, when a van comes from the big city and trays of loaf bread, rock buns and tea cakes are carried into the shop. Hunger grips the village – women in the middle of washing or ironing hurry across, often with their aprons still on, often without the money, eager to collar one of those long soft loaves that are the food of life.

'I'll pay you later' or 'I'll pay you Friday' is often heard as they hasten back to their own kitchens to devour the sacramental fare. In the snug room of the bar, there are already at that hour one or two early topers drinking slowly, methodically, recognizing that the day has just begun, and here too gossip is rife, but in more measured tones. In this dark precinct that smells of porter, old porter and freshly drawn porter, the light is dim because of the fawn blind being permanently drawn, for privacy's sake, and the men, when they at length do decide to address each other, try to escape small matters of their own environment and discuss world topics from items they have gleaned in the newspapers. The furniture here is brown, the counter traced again and again with the circle of the glasses, circles that loop into one another like the circles in the core of a tree.

The loaves of bread that have been snapped up are devoured by housewives at home who lather them with jam or pickles or whatever, anything to give the morning a bit of zest, and soon it's time to put on the dinner and women hurry into their back gardens to cut a head or two of cabbage, then wash it to free it of clay and slugs and put it on to boil for the dinner, which is served midday, usually with bacon. Nice big greasy dinners for some, for others, scraps. Children in front gardens eating bits of bread and sugar, mild activity around lunch-time, people to-ing and fro-ing and the dogs on the village green yelping over a bone or territory or some distemper. Then a lull until tea-time. Older people dozing and from the school window, if it is open, the chants from the children either yelling or reciting in unison.

In the evenings the smell of the yew trees and the pine trees seems to be more pronounced, especially after rain. These grow in profusion in the church grounds, some that were planted many years ago and some that have seeded themselves. Across the road from the church you will see a two-storey stone house, you cannot avoid it. It was once painted blue but is now a dim replica of that colour. The garden is a disgrace. Everything is rampant: trees, shrubs, briars all meshed together in some mad knot, not only obscuring the path, but travelling right up along the windows, so that no one can see in. In there is Ita. Ita was once a paragon in this hamlet, the most admired devout person there. Along with looking after her brother and having a few hens and chickens and milking the cows, she looked after the church; she was the sacristan. The church was at once her sanctuary and her flower garden.

Outside, and due to the inclemency of the weather, the blue cut stone may have imparted a lugubriousness to passersby, but inside all was gleaming, as befits a place which houses God. The sanctuary lamp, perpetually alight, was of Paduan silver hanging low on lattice chains, its bowl pierced with holes containing the inner red bowl in which the sacred oil first glugged, then swayed; here too floated the wick with its tongue of sacred flame bespeaking the presence of Christ. Each time that Ita McNamara stepped inside she not only genuflected, she fell in front of the altar and prayed to God to sweeten her bitter cup, and God did.

It is many years now, but the memory of it is lasting. The missioners were due. The altar had to be sumptuously decked. She did not despair, she knew she would not have to resort to bits of evergreen and shrub because the Protestant spinsters would leave a sheaf of flowers in the porch, ample as a sheaf of corn. They were the only people who gardened, others had not the time or the will for such fal-lalling; others grew potatoes, cabbages and turnips but not flowers or flowering trees; maybe a bit of wild honeysuckle might be found threading its way through the eaves or a few devil's pokers defying the sodden aspect of a forlorn front garden, but a profusion of flowers, no. People had too much to do, trying to keep body and soul together, to eke out an existence. It was June when the catastrophe happened to Ita. 'Satan's net', it was fancifully christened by the cookery teacher who reminded the shocked faithful that many mystics in the Middle Ages had shown such symptoms, and that Ita could have been saved had there been a sensible doctor in the place. Before her downfall, her rhapsody. The flowers that she had been expecting were indeed in the chapel porch, and a prodigal bunch it was. She ran back to her own house to get extra vases, possibly uttering a prayer for the poor heathens, hoping a bolt of lightning would strike them, as it did Saul of Tarsus. Her fears for their damnation were no secret. She confessed once that her own flesh scorched at the thought, that she itched under the armpits and in her joints, it was as if live coals had been placed there, off a tongs. She often asked people to remember them in their prayers, so that they would not be perpetually lost, banished behind the gates of Hell, among the self-loathing, howling hordes.

Ita's brother, who was then alive, saw her pick up three empty jam jars, dump the remains of marmalade that had fungus on it from another jar, rinse it, then pick out the artificial flowers from the rainbow-spiralled vase and run. She took a long time decking the altar. She put the blue and the purple flowers on the altar steps, reserving the white lilies, Mary's flowers, for the altar itself, placing them on either side of the gold-crested tabernacle. The orange flaggers being too flagrant were put in the outer porch near the holy-water font. She stood enraptured, surveying things – the altar cloth like a frosted banner, the white flowers spectral, satin, the pristine beeswax candles, and then other flowers along the steps, where alas those imps of altar boys could kick them or trample on them as they bustled about. She liked none of those boys, infidels at heart, making fun of the parish priest, trying on his vestments, imitating his sing-song voice and the way his eyes rolled upwards of their own accord.

Next day she scrubbed the tiled floor, waxed the woodwork, even waxing the seats where people would plonk their backsides and their wet drapery. Not a cobweb remained in the high corners of the ceiling or in the window casements, no dust along the rim of the confessional doors and ledges and the church doors wide open to let the fresh air pour through. Later, she hauled across the two buckled stepladders, put a plank along the top, rested a chair on that and climbed up, in order to fill the sanctuary lamp with oil. Even her brother feared that she might have a seizure. He insisted that she rest, but no, she had a last chore. She had to make a sponge cake for the missioner, even though she did not know his taste in eats. The missioner the previous year had been elderly and had left them with a dire imprimatur, which was that when in bed they were to fold their arms in the form of a cross and recite:

'I must die, I do not know when, nor how,
Nor where; but if I die in mortal sin
I am lost for ever;
Oh, Jesus, have mercy on me.'

Yes, everything was at the ready, the chapel spick and span, the altar seraphic, the sponge cake filled with lemon curd, sprinkled with sugar, propped on a cake plate and Ita with her long hair drawn back and held with a tortoiseshell slide. If she had any worry, it was the desecration, as such, that the local people would do to the church. She resented them trooping in, enjoying the sight of the flowers, soaking up the missioner's words, lingering afterwards to have a word with him. Many of the farmers smelt awful, smelt of cow-dung and things, but many of the town girls smelt worse, smelt of sin, and Ita knew it. If she had her way she would take these girls, lock them in a dark room, beat them and then starve them to death. One such hussy had the audacity to ask if Ita wanted any help with the altar or if she could perhaps wash the linen. The linen! Her lewd hands touching it, her scrubbing board party to it, a scrubbing board on which filth had been pummelled. Ita slapped her face, slapped her smartly on both cheeks, so much so that word went round that Ita McNamara had gone insane, had lost her marbles.

She went to the parish priest's house after dark, knocked on the side door and spoke to a grump of a maid who did an 'Indeed' as she went down the hall calling 'Father – Father.' The priest met Ita without his stiff collar and was obviously nettled at being disturbed. There were crumbs on his lips, yellow cake crumbs. He listened to her explanation and accepted her offer for a Mass to be said as propitiation. It was a large donation, the money she had put aside to go to Dublin one day. She did not regret it. Her joy in her work was utter, and on the evening before the mission she knelt for a moment surveying her little palace, yielding to a moment of ecstasy. A child who was kneeling in the back of the chapel said she saw Ita McNamara wobble, then she saw her stagger as she held on to the altar rails, then she heard her talk either to herself or to Our Lord or to someone.

So perhaps it had begun then, although others insisted that it began the moment she laid eyes on the missioner himself. He was a young man and came upon her by surprise. He had come into the chapel softly, scarcely making any tread, in his thonged, well-worn sandals. He smiled when he saw what she was doing. From a glass perfume spray, Ita was bathing the faces of the flowers. This thin, delicate-looking priest introduced himself as Father Bonaventure and congratulated her on the beauty of the chapel. He said that one might be at Chartres or Lourdes, so exalting were the surroundings. She thanked him and shuffled away, having registered his rimless spectacles with a half-moon of thicker glass at the bottom of each lens, his commodious robes the colour of bullrushes and his voice gentle yet so incisive, like a diamond cutter.

His sermon on the first evening of the mission began gently, ruminatively; yet no one was misled by that gentleness, least of all the wayward young girls, who sensed the sternness in his being, or the young men, who bristled at his scrutiny as he asked them to lift the veil and look into their souls and consider if by evil ways or evil thoughts they were crucifying afresh their loving Saviour, putting through the most holy soul of Mary the shaft of a sword, a shaft similar to that which passed through her in the hours of the Passion. His voice carried. It issued through the open windows, so that the Protestants doing a bit of gardening could hear it, as could the dumb beasts, the braying donkeys with gnats clotted on their eyelids, as could the little tufts of cowslips or primroses and every growing thing.

It was Ita who tended to him later, got some glucose and a glass of water. It seems he slumped on a bench in the sacristy, beads of sweat on his lips and on his temples accusing himself of not having moved the faithful enough. He resembled some great performer who feared that he had lost his touch with his audience. His assistant, a far younger priest, Father Finbar, was outside in the chapel grounds, bidding the people good night. Father Finbar, who had pinkish skin rather like a girl's, did not of course give sermons, but would be called on to assist at the Rosary and the Benediction and would probably hear some of the confessions. Later the two priests left together, their horn rosaries swaying against the folds of their brown robes and their hoods pulled up because it had begun to spatter with rain. They walked in silence over the path where the trod-on berries from the yew trees were like drops of blood, and then they went along the main road that was deserted now because of all the people having gone home. Ita watched them, and some children who were playing hide-and-seek saw what she did, then tattled about it. She picked up a cake box that was inside the gate to her house and ran after them, at a gallop. They had stopped at a bend on the road to look at a herd of fawn cattle, in a field. She thrust the box into Father Bonaventure's hands and came away blushing. She put her finger to her lips by way of exacting secrecy from the children, and gave them a penny between them.

Confessions were heard each morning and the entire parish was enjoined to go. Ita watched them like a hawk each year because some were bound to cheat. A wicked or a cunning person could go up, kneel down, but at the last moment refuse the Host and yet return with eyes devoutly closed, as if the Host were dissolving. Just after the first two people had gone in to confess, an incident occurred. A girl by the name of Nancy fainted, fainted in high operatic manner, so that her arms slapped onto those next to her and her missal with all its contents scattered over the aisle; holy pictures with far from holy inscriptions were seen and read by several. The upshot was that this girl Nancy could not go in to confess, had to be carried to the harness-maker's nearby and be given a spoon of tonic wine in hot water. Ita, sensing foul play, commandeered the girl's younger sister, Della, brought Della out to the chapel grounds and quizzed her inordinately about her sister's behaviour. Was Nancy out late at night? Was Nancy seeing some boy? Was Nancy off her food in the morning and complaining of nausea? In short, was Nancy in a state of mortal sin and possibly having a baby? Another blight on their village.

The little girl Della got so frightened at this inquisition that to divert things she put the palm of her hand on the spear of the railing and threatened to gouge herself, to do penance for the whole world, her sister included. Ita gave her a sound thumping then and sent her back into the church. Many overheard it and wondered why Ita had become so officious. She quarrelled with several local people, but particularly with the parish priest's housekeeper, since the missioners were staying there, tackled her about menus, told her to buck up and give them something better than packet soup and synthetic jelly set with boiled milk to give it a bit of fuzz. Later people were quick to insist that yes, they had noticed it then but they had thought it was a temporary aberration.

She spent far more hours than was necessary in the church, laying out several vestments for the priest, separating each of the altar breads in such a manner that when they were put in the chalice the priest could pick each one up separately and easily. She used the excuse to be in the church all the time by polishing the floor again and again, so much so that people skeetered over it, and once she was heard humming to herself and it was not a hymn, more like a refrain. Because of the crush in the church for the evening sermons – all were obliged to go and mostly all did – people had to be accommodated behind the altar rails, lined up along the altar steps, and usually it was children who were put there and usually it was the sacristan who organized it. No longer. Ita selected who would go in there and then sat among them, directly gazing up at the priest, catching the words, the incendiary words as they formed in his mouth just before he uttered them. Father Bonaventure, who had been gentle on the first evening, grew fiercer with each sermon, expatiating on the fires of Hell, the loss of the sight of God, the absence of grace, and reminding them of their last, perhaps their very last chance for redemption. At certain moments he foamed. He spared no one. He paused between words and sentences, to look into faces, the faces of those clustered around him including Ita, the gnarled faces of the older people in the pews with their heads bent, the shamed faces of the men standing at the back, and to each of them, it was as if he spoke directly and clairvoyantly. Then, fearing he had gone too far, he appealed to them. He softened his words and reminded them that if they persisted in their mortifications God would respond, and His pent-up fountain of love and mercy would burst open to grant their wishes.

Emotion was rampant. People quaked with terror, others made vows out loud, others thumped their chests, others moaned, all except Ita, who gazed at him, glorious, beatific, triumphant, no longer the awkward creature, but now an almost presentable woman with a beret which she wore at an angle. People had remarked about this because Ita had always worn a headscarf and pulled it so far forward that it shelved on either side of her face. But here she was, inside the altar rails, gazing at the priest, her black angora beret at an angle, her cheeks adorned with rouge. At least some swore it was rouge though others said it was flush from the blaze of the candles.

At his last sermon, so fervid was he, so resonant the vibrations of his words, that a lily, a white flute, fell stealthily off its stalk, onto the altar cloth. The people shivered, all hearkening to his strictures. The 'terrene affections', as he called them, had to be crushed in favour of the love of the Almighty and the camaraderie of Christ. Many saw the lily, its white skin shrivelling in the heat, its yellow stamen specking the altar cloth, but then it was just a lily, a fallen inert thing.

When the faithful had gone, Ita had many tasks to do. She had to put away the cruets and the silver for the next year's mission, throw out the withered flowers and put the good ones on the tiled floor of the sacristy, far away from the fumes of the quenched candles. Moreover, people were pestering her with requests to have a word with Father Bonaventure, alone. Some thought that a private word with him would grant them unheard-of indulgences. The little nitwit Della asked if she could have her autograph book signed, and for her impertinence got a biff. All the while Father Bonaventure was behind the screen changing from his embroidered vestments into the brown robes of his order. Sometime during that bustle, Ita must have taken the lily flute and put it in her pocket; maybe she thought to place it under her pillow, in the way that young girls put the crumbs of a wedding cake there, to dream of their betrothed. Della swears that Ita was crying, but then the mission made many people cry as they came face to face with the gravity of things. No one actually saw her and Father Bonaventure say goodbye. Many are divided about the hour of his departure. Some say he dallied, while others insist that he left almost immediately. The stall owners, who had tents outside the chapel gates, had already gone, and the mother-of-pearl rosaries, the fulsome leaflets, the blessed scapulars and all the other sacred impedimenta were in boxes, waiting to be despatched to the seaside town where Father Bonaventure was due to preach.

Ita went home, and as her dismayed brother was later to attest, she behaved quite normally. He admitted to having been rather ratty with her on account of her being so late, he himself had driven a few crippled people home from the mission and was still back half an hour before she appeared. The fire was out, as he said, and he had to coax it back to life with newspaper and paraffin. She seemed to him no different than usual except that she refused to eat, vowing that she would be fasting from now on. Those hours mark the divide between the Ita that everyone knew and the lunatic that was to emerge and be dragged out of there at cockcrow.

Villagers were sunk in sleep, even dogs that barked and marauded on the green had quietened down, when a roar followed by a volley of roars shook the village. It being summertime, most people had their windows open. Ita's brother heard it, of course, as did the nearest neighbours, who jumped out of their beds believing there was a robbery or that the tinkers were on the rampage again. People with coats or cardigans flung over them were seen running, and soon they were in Ita's room witnessing the crazed sight of her sitting up in bed, her nightdress bundled up around her middle as she wept copiously. Her brother asked if it was bats, as he lit a stump of a candle. Often on the summer nights bats came in, cleaved to the ceiling or the rim of a ewer, and then swooped about once it was dark. 'Not bats ... not bats,' she said, pointing to the lily, which was the cause of her dementia. It lay beside her on the bed, close to the calf of her leg, which was full of scratches. It had moved. It had taken flesh. It was dirty. They must get Father Bonaventure, because only he could exorcise it.

'Keep back ... keep back,' she said as her brother tried

to pluck it from her. She had now withdrawn to the head of the bed, her black hair splayed on the wrought iron. Her eyes were wild too. She got it into her head that they were all against her, and cursed them from the fortress of her bed. The cookery teacher tried to calm her, told her how much they all loved her and asked if she would like a cup of tea. Then she reminded everyone of Ita's Trojan work during the mission and said that most likely she was exhausted. The praise softened her ire, and breaking into a childlike smile Ita blessed herself and said, 'Blessed is he that is not scandalized in me.' They knew now that it was in earnest and that she was talking heresy. Her moods altered between states of near beatitude and begging to be beaten, to be scourged alive. Her brother said that was what was needed and dashed out of the room to get his ash plant but the neighbours remonstrated with him, said she must have the priest because she was possessed.

While he was gone, Ita treated them to some strange tales and used swear words that they did not know were in her vocabulary. She described the assault of the lily, how it ran out from under the pillow, crawled all over her like a hairy Molly and was impervious to grasp. Yes, it was the Devil, she knew that. Then she expressed a doubt and said it was not the Devil; then she tore at her flesh again, which was already full of cuts, and asked them to pray that she could be redeemed. Yet when Father Bonaventure arrived she acted like a courtesan, put her hand out to welcome him, said to excuse her 'deshabille', adding that her stockings were in flitters. Then she asked to be left alone with him and spoke in a whisper. She made mention of their days together, the promises they had made, and how they were going abroad as a team to convert heathens. Each time he accused her of imagining things she flared up and asked him to look at her body, to look at where Satan had been, to drive the serpent away, to crush it with his thumbs or his sandalled foot or his beads. He did not wish to look at her body. With one hand she grabbed him and with the other held the candleholder slant-wise over the thin matt of greying hair and asked did he not see it? She said he must see it. It was there. It was a blister of blood, Christ's blood, and had blood as its essence. She had been with Christ. Oh yes, he knew, but he was jealous, wanting her for himself. Who now was the culprit clinging to 'terrene affections', begging for her love? Who now but him? Immediately he began to pray rapidly and summoned the others in from the landing to pray with him, and so great was her rage at his calling for witnesses that she put the candle first to the sleeve of her nightdress, then to the matt of hair where she had been taken in adultery. But who were they to throw stones? Quick to smell the scorching, a youngster came from the kitchen with a pitcher of water which was poured over her. Ita laughed and said she felt like a little girl, remembered her youth, the daisy chains she had made and a game she played tracing a penny onto a page.

Very early, she was brought to the asylum, where she spent the best part of a year and took to sucking in her cheeks, refusing to speak to anyone and having to be barred from the chapel because the sight of flowers drove her into a frenzy. She took up smoking too, and the authorities indulged her in that, thinking it would take her mind off her troubles. She cadged cigarettes off visitors and told some very tall tales about travels she had made in the Far East, where she was a nursing sister and where she had contracted malaria. In about a year, when she was calm with tablets and shock treatment, they brought her home, and from then on she avoided people, growling at anyone who spoke to her, even the priest or the doctor. Being alone now, she does the farm work and has taken to wearing her brother's old clothes and Wellington boots. She is always forking manure, or washing out the cow house, or carrying buckets of feed and water up the hills to the store cattle. 'There goes the one with the roastings,' people say. She is like a landmark, one bucket in either hand, either going up the hill or returning to have them refilled. Children say that she curses them, and those who knock on her door are likely to be met with a pitchfork or a saucepan of hot stirabout.

Now I ask you, what would you do? Would you comfort Ita, would you tell her that her sins were of her own imagining; then might you visit the budding beauty and set her dreaming of the metropolis, would you loiter with the drunkards and laugh with the women gorging the white bread, would you perhaps visit the grave to say an Ave where Angela, her sister and the errant husband lie close together, morsels for the maggots, or would you drive on helter-skelter, the radio at full blast. Perhaps your own village is much the same, perhaps everywhere is, perhaps pity is a luxury and deliverance a thing of the past.

BROTHER

BAD CESS TO HIM. Thinks I don't know, that I didn't smell a rat. All them bachelors swaggering in here, calling him out to the haggart in case I twigged. 'Tutsy this and Tutsy that.' A few readies in it for them, along with drives and big feeds. They went the first Sunday to reconnoitre, walk the land and so forth. The second Sunday they went in for refreshments. Three married sisters, all gawks. If they're not hitched up by now there must be something wrong; hare lip or a limp or fits. He's no oil painting, of course. Me doing everything for him; making his porridge and emptying his worshipful po, for God knows how many years. Not to mention his lumbago, and the liniment I rubbed in.

'I'll be good to you, Maisie,' he says. Good! A bag of toffees on a holy day. Takes me for granted. All them fly-boys at threshing time trying to ogle me up into the loft for a fumble. Puckauns. I'd take a pitchfork to any one of them; so would he if he knew. I scratched his back many's the night and rubbed the liniment on it. Terrible aul smell. Eucalyptus.

'Lower . . . lower,' he'd say. 'Down there.' Down to the puddingy bits, the lupins. All to get to my Mary. He had a Mass said in the house after. Said he saw his mother, our mother; something on her mind. I had to have grapefruit for the priest's breakfast, had to de-pip it. These priests are real gluttons. He ate in the breakfast room and kept admiring things in the cabinet, the china bell and the bog-oak cabin, and so forth. Thought I'd part with them. I was running in and out with hot tea, hot water, hot scones; he ate enough for three. Then the big handshake; Matt giving him a tenner. I never had that amount in my whole life. Ten bob on Fridays to get provisions, including sausages for his breakfast. Woeful the way he never consulted me. He began to get hoity-toity, took off that awful trousers with the greasy backside from all the sweating and lathering on horseback, tractor and bike; threw it in the fire cavalier-like. Had me airing a suit for three days. I had it on a clothes-horse, turning it round every quarter of an hour, for fear of it scorching.

Then the three bachelors come into the yard again, blabbing about buying silage off him. They had silage to burn. It stinks the countryside. He put on his cap and went out to talk to them. They all leant on the gate, cogitating. I knew 'twas fishy, but it never dawned on me it could be a wife. I'd have gone out and sent them packing. Talking low they were, and at the end they all shook hands. At the supper he said he was going to Galway Sunday.

'What's in Galway?' I said.

'A greyhound,' he said.

First mention of a greyhound since our little Deirdre died. The pride and joy of the parish she was. Some scoundrels poisoned her. I found her in a fit outside in the shed, yelps coming out of her, and foam. It nearly killed him. He had a rope that he was ruminating with, for months. Now this bombshell. Galway.

'I'll come with you, I need a sea breeze,' I said.

'It's all male, it's stag,' he said and grinned.

I might have guessed. Why they were egging him on I'll never know, except 'twas to spite me. Some of them have it in for me; I drove bullocks of theirs off our land, I don't give them any haults on bonfire night. He went up to the room then and wouldn't budge. I left a slice of griddle bread with golden syrup on it outside the door. He didn't touch it. At dawn I was raking the ashes and he called me, real soft-soapy, 'Is that you Maisie, is that you?' Who in blazes' name did he think it was – Bridget or Mary of the gods! 'Come in for a minute,' he said, 'there's a flea or some goddamn thing itching me, maybe it's a tick, maybe they've nested.' I strip the covers and in th'oul candlelight he's like one of those saints that they boil, thin and raky. Up to then I only ventured in the dark, on windy nights when he'd say he heard a ghost and I had to go to him. I reconnoitre his white body while he's muttering on about the itch, says, 'Soldiers in the tropics minded itch more than combat.' He read that in an almanac.

'Maisie,' he says in a watery voice, and puts his hand on mine and steers me to his shorthorn. Pulled the stays off of me. Thinking I don't know what he was after. All pie. Raving about me being the best sister in the wide world and I'd give my last shilling and so forth. Talked about his young days when he hunted with a ferret. Babble, babble. His limbs were like jelly, and then the grunts and him burying himself under the red flannel eiderdown, saying God would strike us.

The next Sunday he was off again. Not a word to me since the tick mutiny, except to order me to drive cattle or harness the horse. Got a new pullover, a most unfortunate colour, like piccalilli. He didn't get home that Sunday until all hours. I heard the car door banging. He boiled himself milk, because the saucepan was on the range with the skin on it. I went up to the village to get meal for the hens and everyone was gassing about it. My brother had got engaged for the second time in two weeks. First it was a Dymphna and now it was a Tilly. It seemed he was in their parlour – pictures of cows and millstreams on the wall – sitting next to his intended, eating cold ox-tongue and beetroot, when he leans across the table, points to Tilly and says, 'I think I'd sooner her.'

Uproar. They all dropped utensils and gaped at him, thinking it a joke. He sticks to his guns, so much so that her father and the bachelors drag him out into the garden for a heart-to-heart. Garden. It seems it's only high grass and an obelisk that wobbles. They said, 'What the Christ, Matt?' He said, 'I prefer Tilly, she's plumper.' Tilly was called out and the two of them were told to walk down to the gate and back, to see what they had in common.

In a short time they return and announce that they understand one another and wish to be engaged. Gink. She doesn't know the catastrophe she's in for. She doesn't know about me and my status here. Dymphna had a fit, shouted, threw bits of beetroot and gizzard all about and said, 'My sister is a witch.' Had to be carried out and put in a box-room, where she shrieked and banged with a set of fire-irons that were stored there. Parents didn't care, at least they were getting one cissy off their hands. Father breeds French herds, useless at it. A name like Charlemagne. The bachelors said Matt was a brave man, drink was mooted. All the arrangements that had been settled on Dymphna were now transferred to Tilly. My brother drank port wine and got maudlin. Hence the staggers in the yard when he got home and the loud octavias. Never said a word at the breakfast. I had to hear it in the village. She has mousey hair and one of her eyes squints, but instead of calling it a squint the family call it a 'lazy eye'. It is to be a quiet wedding. He hasn't asked me, he won't. Thinks I'm too much of a gawk with my gap teeth, and that I'd pass remarks and say, 'I've eaten to my satisfaction and if I ate any more I'd go flippety-floppety,' a thing he makes me say here to give him a rise in the wet evenings.

All he says is 'There'll be changes, Maisie, and it's for the best.' Had the cheek to ask me to make an eiderdown for the bed, rose-coloured satin. I'll probably do it, but it will only be a blind. He thinks I'm a softie. I'll be all pie to her at first, bringing her the tea in bed and asking her if she'd like her hair done with the curling tongs. We'll pick elderflowers to make jelly. She'll be in a shroud before the year is out. To think that she's all purty now, like a little bower bird, preening herself. She won't even have the last rites. I've seen a photo of her. She sent it to him for under his pillow. I'll take a knife to her, or a hatchet. I've been in Our Lady's once before, it isn't that bad. Big teas on Sundays and fags. I'll be out in a couple of years. He'll be so morose from being all alone, he'll welcome me back with open arms. It's human nature. It stands to reason. The things I did for him, going to him in the dark, rubbing in that aul liniment, washing out at the rain barrel together, mother-naked, my bosoms slapping against him, the stars fading and me bursting my sides with the things he said – 'Dotey'. Dotey no less. I might do for her out of doors. Lure her to the waterfall to look for eggs. There're swans up there and geese. He loves the big geese eggs. I'll get behind her when we're on that promontory and give her a shove. It's very slippery from the moss. I can just picture her going down, yelling, then not yelling, being swept away like a newspaper or an empty canister. I'll call the alarm. I'll shout for him. If they do smell a rat and tackle me, I'll tell them that I could feel beads of moisture on my brother's poll without even touching it, I was that close to him. There's no other woman could say that, not her, not any woman. I'm all he has, I'm all he'll ever have. Roll on, nuptials. Daughter of death is she.

THE WIDOW

BRIDGET WAS HER NAME. She played cards like a trooper, and her tipple was gin-and-lime. She kept lodgers, but only select lodgers: people who came for the dapping, or maybe a barrister who would come overnight to discuss a case with a client or with a solicitor.

The creamery manager was the first guest to be more or less permanent. After a few months it was clear he wasn't going to build the bungalow that he had said he would, and after a few more months he was inviting girls to the house as if it were his own. Oh the stories, the stories! Card parties, drink, and God knows what else. No one dared ask expressly. Gaudy women, with nail varnish, and lizard handbags and so forth, often came, sometimes staying for the weekend. Bridget had devoted the sitting room to him and his guests, choosing to say that whatever they wanted to do was their business.

She worked in the daytime, in a local shop, where she was a bookkeeper. She kept herself very much to herself – sat in her little office with its opaque beaded-glass panelling, and wrote out the bills and paid for commodities, and rarely, if ever, came out to the shop to serve customers.

The owner and she got on well. He called her Biddy, short for Bridget, which meant, of course, that they were good friends. Occasionally she would emerge from her glass booth to congratulate a young mother on having a baby or to sympathize with someone over a death, but this, as people said, was a formality, a mere gesture. No one had been invited to her new pebble-dash house, and the twin sisters who called unannounced were left standing on the doorstep, with some flimsy excuse about her distempering the kitchen ceiling. She was determined to remain aloof, and as if to emphasize the point she had Venetian blinds fitted.

You may ask, as the postmistress had asked – the postmistress her sworn enemy – 'Why have Venetian blinds drawn at all times, winter and summer, daylight and dark? What is Bridget trying to hide?' What went on there at night, after she strolled home, carrying a few tasties that the owner of the shop had given her, such as slices of bacon or tins of salmon? It was rumoured that she changed from her dark shop overall into brighter clothes. A child had seen her carrying in a scuttle of coal. So there was a fire in the parlour, people were heard to say.

Parties began to take place, and many a night a strange car or two, or even three, would park outside her driveway and remain there till well near dawn. Often people were heard emerging, singing 'She'll be comin' 'round the mountain when she comes, when she comes.' Such frivolities inevitably lead to mishaps, and there came one that stunned the parish. A priest died in the house. He was not a local priest but had arrived in one of those strange cars with strange registration numbers. The story was that he went up to the bathroom, missed a step as he came out, and then, of course – it could happen to anyone – tripped and fell. He fell all the way down the fifteen steps of stairs, smashed his head on the grandfather clock that was at the bottom, and lay unconscious on the floor. The commotion was something terrible, as Rita, a neighbour, reported. There were screams from inside the house. The creamery manager, it seems, staggered to his car, but was too inebriated to even start the engine; then a young lady followed, drove off, and shortly after the local curate arrived at the house with the viaticum. An hour later, the ambulance brought the priest to the hospital, but he was already dead.

Bridget put a brave face on it. Instead of hiding her understandable guilt, she acknowledged it. She spoke over and over again of the fatal night, the fun that had preceded the tragedy, the priest, not touching a drop, regaling them with the most wonderful account of being admitted to the Vatican – not for an audience, as he had thought, but to see the treasures. 'Thousands of pounds' worth of treasures ... thousands of pounds' worth of treasures!' he had apparently said as he described a picture or a sculpture or a chalice or vestments. Then Bridget would go on to describe how they had all played a game of forty-five and before they knew where they were it was three in the morning and Father So-and-So rose to return home, going upstairs first. He had had, as she said, glass after glass of lemonade. Then the terrible thud, and their not believing what it was, and the creamery manager getting up from the table and going out to the hall, and then a girl going out, and then the screams. Bridget made it known that she would never forgive herself for not having had a stronger bulb on the landing. At the High Mass for the priest's remains, she wore a long black lace thing, which she had not taken out since her beloved husband had died.

Her husband had been drowned years before, which is why she was generally known as the Widow. They had been married only a few months and were lovebirds. They had lived in another house then – a little house with a porch that caught the sun, where they grew geraniums and begonias and even a few tomatoes. Her despair at his death was so terrible it was legendary. Her roar, when the news was broken to her, rent the parish, and was said to have been heard in distant parishes. Babies in their cots heard it, as did old people who were deaf and sitting beside the fire, as did the men working out in the fields. When she was told that her husband had drowned she would not believe it: her husband was not dead; he was a strong swimmer; he swam down at the docks every evening of his life before his tea. She rebelled by roaring. She roared all that evening and all that night. Nobody in the village could sleep. When they found his body in the morning with reeds matted around it, her cries reached a gargantuan pitch. She could not be let to go to the chapel. Women held her down to keep her from going berserk.

Then, some days after he was buried, when the cattle began to trample over the grave and treat it as any old grave, she stopped her keening. Soon after, she put on a perfectly calm, cheerful, resigned countenance. She told everyone that she was a busy woman now and had much to do. She had to write to thank all the mourners, and thank the priests who officiated at the High Mass, and then decide what to do about her husband's clothes. Above all, she was determined to sell her house. She was advised against it, but nothing would deter her. That house was for Bill and herself – 'Darling Bill', as she called him – and only by leaving it would the memory, the inviolate memory, of their mornings and their evenings and their nights and their tête-à-têtes remain intact.

She sold the house easily, though far too cheaply, and went back to the country to live with her own folks – a brother and a deaf-mute sister. No one in the village heard of her until a few years later, when her brother died and her sister went to an institution. Unable to manage the tillage and foddering, Bridget sold the farm and moved back to the town. She was a changed woman when she came back – very much more in charge of herself. Very much more the toff, as people said. She got a job as a bookkeeper in the shop and started to build a house, and while it was being built many conjectured that she had a second husband in mind. There were rumours about bachelors seen talking to her, and especially one who came from America and took her to the dog track in Limerick a few Saturday nights in a row and bought her gins. The news of her drinking soon spread, and the verdict was that she could bend the elbow with any man. Hence, being installed in her new house was not the neighbourly affair it might have been. There was no housewarming, for instance; no little gifts of cream or homemade black puddings or porter cake; no good-luck horseshoe on her door. In short, the people ostracized her. She seemed not to mind, having always kept to herself anyway. She had a good wardrobe, she had a good job, and as soon as she started to keep select boarders – only two, or at the most three – everybody remarked that she was getting above herself. Her house was sarcastically called the Pleasure Dome, and sometimes, more maliciously, she was coupled with the song 'Biddy the Whore, who lived in a hotel without any door'.

Her first two guests were strangers – men who were doing some survey for the land commission, and whom all the farmers suspected of being meddlesome. They and Bridget became the best of friends – sat outside on deck chairs and were heard laughing; went to Mass together, the last Mass on Sundays; and in the evening imbibed, either at home or in the hotel. When they left, the creamery manager arrived – a big man with wide shoulders and a large, reddish face. He was voluble, affectionate. He touched people's lapels, particularly women's, and he was not shy about asking for a kiss. A few of the girls professed to have spurned him. The old maids, who mistrusted him, watched him when he left the creamery at half past five in the evening to see if he would go straight to his lodgings or across to the town to have a pint or two. They would lie in wait behind walls, or behind the windows of their sitting rooms. He rarely mentioned Bridget by name but referred to her as the Landlady, often adding how saucy she was, and what a terrific cook. He was especially fond of her lamb stew, which, as people said, was really mutton stew.

Soon the creamery manager, whose name was Michael, acquired a steady girlfriend called Mea. Mea was a bank clerk from the city, and she came in her car at weekends and stayed two nights. He would splash himself with eau de cologne on the evenings she was expected, and was to be seen traipsing in front of the house, so eager was he to see her. They never kissed on the steps but always went inside and left some of the local snoopers, especially the women, demented with curiosity as to what happened next. She could, as Bridget told the shopkeeper, who then told it to everyone else, twist Michael around her little finger. She was subject, it seemed, to the most fitful moods – sometimes bright as a hummingbird, other times professing to have a headache or a sinus or a stomach ache, and refusing even to speak to him. Once, she locked herself in her bedroom and did not come out for the whole evening. She ate like a bird, bleached her hair with egg yolk and lemon, and cut a great dash at Mass or devotions, always managing to have a different hat or a different headscarf each Sunday. It was noticed that she hardly prayed at all – that she looked around, summing up the people, sneering at them – and that she was not certain when were the times to stand and when were the times to kneel, but would look around to gauge what others were doing.

'Ah, it's her sweet mystery ... her sweet mystery,' Michael had told Bridget, who had told the shopkeeper, who had, of course, told others. Before long, Mea and Michael were engaged, and Mea was coming not only two nights a week but three nights a week, and driving all around with him to see if there were any uninhabited houses or bungalows, because of course they would want their own place. Each week, as well, she bought some item of furniture, usually something bulky – a mirror or a wardrobe or a whatnot or a bureau – and he was heard to say that she was furniture-mad. In jest he would ask the men why he was putting a rope around his neck.

They were to be married in June, but one evening early in May there was a rift. Michael broke it off. It happened at the hotel, just as the crowd was wishing them well and making innuendos about the patter of little feet. Michael was very drunk – his drinking had got heavy over the past few weeks – and suddenly he turned to Mea and said, very candidly and almost tearfully, that he could not go through with it. She was to keep the ring; he wanted everything to end in good faith. She slapped him, there and then, three times on the cheek in front of everyone. 'How dare you,' she said with the acerbity of a governess, and then she ran out and he followed, and soon they drove off down the Shannon Road – no doubt to patch things up, as people said. But Michael was adamant. The engagement was broken off.

She left that night, and Michael hid for three days. He went back to the creamery, drawn and unshaven, and on that Friday he learned of her suit for breach of promise by reading of it in the weekly newspaper. There were photos of him and Mea, mention of some little lovey-dovey exchanges, and even a photo of Bridget, who Mea said had had too much influence over him and was probably responsible for the rift. Mea also talked about her broken heart, the several plans she had made, the house that she envisaged, the little rose garden, then discussed her bottom drawer, which was full of linen and lavender sachets and so on. Above all, she bemoaned the fact that her romantic future with any other man was out of the question; in short, that her life was destroyed. Michael received a solicitor's letter, consulted his local solicitor, and was said to have paid her a hefty compensation. Then he went on the batter for a few weeks and was carted to the Cistercian monastery, and finally came home looking thinner and much more subdued. 'A gold-digger, a gold-digger, that's what she was,' Bridget would say whenever Mea's name was mentioned, and in time the matter was forgotten.

It was perceived – first by the postmistress, then by another woman, who spoke about it to several others – that Bridget and the creamery manager were flirting openly. Soon after, they were seen holding hands as they took a walk down the Chapel Road after Benediction. They had lingered in the chapel, allowing the others to leave. It was the sacristan who saw them, and ran and told it in the town, once she had recovered from her fright. People asked if she was certain, or if she had not imagined it. 'That I may drop dead if it's not true,' she said, putting her hand to the grey wool cardigan that covered her sunken bosom.

The inappropriateness of this was more than they could stomach. After all, she was a widow, and she was a woman in her forties, who ought to know better. Neighbours began to watch more carefully, especially at night, to see how many lights went on in the upstairs rooms – to see if they had separate bedrooms or were living in mortal sin. The less censorious said it was a flash in the pan and soon he would have another beauty in tow, so that all, all were flabbergasted the morning Bridget stood in the doorway of the shop and announced her engagement. To prove it, a lozenge of blue shimmered on her finger, and her eyes were dancing as the people gaped at her.

Before long, Bridget bought a car, and Michael gave her driving lessons on the Dock Road, the very road where her husband had walked to his death. He stopped soliciting young girls, even the young buttermaker in the creamery, and told strangers how happy he was, and that up to now all the women he had known were mere bonbons, and that this was *It*.

Her happiness was too much for people to take; they called her a hussy, they predicted another breach of promise, they waited for the downfall. Some of the older women went to the parish priest about it, but when they arrived the parish priest was in such a grump about the contributions towards a new altar that he told them to pull their socks up and try to raise money by selling cakes and jellies and things at a bazaar. He suspected why they had come, because the creamery manager had gone to him alone, and stayed an hour, and no doubt gave him a substantial offering for Masses.

To put a good complexion on the engagement period, a youngster was brought to Bridget's house from the country, a boy so daft that he dug up the tubers of the irises in mistake for onions – in short, no chaperon. They were to be married in December, which left Bridget two months to pack up her job and prepare her trousseau. She was always to be seen flying in her red car now, a menace to pedestrians and cattle that strayed on the roadside. To ingratiate herself, as they said, she offered people lifts to the city, or offered to do errands for them. Some, being weak, accepted these favours, but not the diehards. A few of the men, it is true, praised her, said what spunk she had. She was much older than Michael, and moreover, she had got him off the booze; he drank only wine now – table wine.

A week before the wedding, the pair went to the local

pub, which they had got out of the habit of doing, and stood drinks to everyone. The shopkeeper, proposing the toast, said he knew that Biddy and Michael had everyone's blessing. People clapped, then someone sang. Then Biddy, being a little tipsy, tapped her glass with her engagement stone and said she was going to give a little recitation. Without further ado, she stood up, smiled that sort of urchin smile of hers, ran her tongue over her lips, another habit, and recited a poem entitled 'People Will Talk'. It was a lunge at all those mischievous, withered people who begrudged her her little flourish. It may have been – indeed, many people said that it was – this audacious provocation that wreaked the havoc of the next weeks. Had she confided in a few local women, she might have been saved, but she did not confide; she stood aloof with her man, her eyes gleaming, her happiness assured.

It never came to light who exactly had begun it, but suddenly the word went round, the skeleton that had been lurking for years – that her husband had not drowned by accident, he had taken his own life. His predicament, it was said, was so grinding that he saw no way out of it. He went down to the docks that evening, after yet another hideous row with her, pen and paper in his pocket, and wrote his farewell note. It was in his trousers pocket before they handed it to her. Why else had she roared for three days, they asked, and why was she unfit to attend her own husband's funeral or the High Mass? Why else did she recover so soon, but that she was a wicked, heartless harlot? The creamery manager, they predicted, would be a scape-goat once the marriage vows were exchanged. First one person whispered it, then another, and then another; the story slipped from house to house, from mouth to mouth, and before long it reached Bridget's appalled ears. As if that were not shock enough, she received one morning an anonymous letter saying that her husband-to-be would know of her skeleton shortly. She flung the letter into the stove, then tried in vain to retrieve it. Luckily, Michael was still upstairs, asleep in his own room. It was then that she made her first mistake – she ran around trying to bribe people, asking them not to mention this terrible rumour, not to tell the creamery manager, for God's sake not to tell. The more she tried to quash the talk, the more people concluded her guilt. She lost all composure. She could be seen in her bare feet or in her nightgown running up the road to meet the postman, to ward off any other dreadful bulletins.

After that morning, she dared not let Michael go anywhere alone, in case someone told him. She knew, or at least clung to the belief, that no one at work would risk telling him, for fear of being fired on the spot. But in the street or on the way to Mass or at the pub – these were the danger zones, and for weeks she followed him everywhere, so that he began to show signs of impatience and said that she was a hairy Molly, clinging to him. Her looks, which had improved since the engagement, took a turn for the worse, and she was what she once had been – a scraggy older woman, with thin hair and skin that was much too yellow.

Michael saw that she was distraught, but did not understand it. It seems he told the young buttermaker that his missus had got the jitters and the sooner they got married the better. Even while he was saying this, his missus-to-be was grasping at any straw. She confided in the shopkeeper, who advised her to tell Michael, but she broke down and even flared up, mistrusting her one friend. 'Why not take the bull by the horns and tell him straight out?' he had said. She couldn't. He would jilt her. Had he not already jilted a younger and comelier girl, and was she, Bridget, not haunted by that same prospect? It was then that she remembered the old woman who have lived across the road from her husband and herself and had later moved back to the country. She would go to find this woman, who would swear that she had never heard a voice raised, and that in fact Bridget and her first husband used to sit in the sun porch in the evening, among the geraniums and the begonias, whispering, holding hands, canoodling.

Then a little respite came. Michael decided to go home to his own folks for a week, and that was a godsend. They would then meet in Limerick, with a small sprinkling of relatives, and there they would be married in the Augustinian church. One of the friars was a friend of Michael's, and he had already made the arrangements. Because of the breach-of-promise episode, it was going to be a very hushed-up affair.

Before leaving, Michael tackled her. He sat her in the little armchair by the kitchen stove, where they had often, so often, joked and cuddled. He asked her if perhaps she was having second thoughts about things, if perhaps she did not love him. Her eyes filled up with tears. She said, 'No, no, Michael . . . no.' She was so in love, she confessed, that she was afraid that it would go wrong. Then he kissed her and reproved her for being a daft little hen of a woman, and they waltzed around the kitchen, promising things that they would do when they were married, like putting a skylight in the kitchen, and getting a new range so that she did not have to dirty her fingers with the ashes and clinkers. He loved her little hands, he said, and he kissed them. 'Num, num,' he said, as if he were eating them, as if they were jam tarts.

As she told the shopkeeper later, they had a blissful farewell. He tried to coax out of her what she was planning to wear at the wedding, but she sang dumb. 'I sang dumb,' she said, and described how she ran upstairs to get the old fox collar, with its little foxy snout and beady eyes, and threatened him with it, went 'Yap, yap, yap.' They played hide-and-seek, they laughed, they teased one another, but on no account would she allow him into the room where her trousseau was stored – her voile gown and her satin shoes, and her piles of new undies, and the fleecy bed jacket. Their farewell was so tender that Michael even debated if he should cancel his journey. 'God blast it, I'm over twenty-one,' he said. But she persuaded him to go, insisted. She knew it was essential that he be away from this place, where any mischief-maker could say, 'I believe your intended wife drove her first husband to his death.' She could not risk it. There was something about Michael, although she never told him this, that reminded her of her first husband. They were both childlike and affectionate, and they both had gruff tempers but were quick to apologize – to lay a bar of chocolate or a hanky on the pillow as an appeasement. She loved them in much the same way – the same gushing, bubbly, childish way that she had loved at twenty – and miraculously, her love was reciprocated.

The day after he left, Bridget set out to see the old woman. She was cheerful in the town when she stopped to buy petrol. She even told the young attendant that she was thinking of throwing a party, and asked if he would like to come. 'Deffo,' was what he claimed to have said.

No one of us ever knew what ensued with the old woman, because it was on the way back that it happened. It was a treacherous bit of road, always known to be; it twisted, then straightened, and then forked suddenly and ridged under a thick canopy of beech trees. Lorries and cars had crashed there so often that people said there was a curse on that stretch. A witch had once lived nearby – a witch who defied the hierarchy and concocted pagan cures from herbs. People wondered if the aftermath of this witch was not the cause of all these disasters, and holy water had been sprinkled there many a time by the priests.

It was after dark when the accident happened. Bridget had gone to the old woman, and afterwards had gone to a hotel in the nearest town and treated herself to a drink. It may have been that she went to the hotel to celebrate, to taste for the first time the joy, as well as the certainty, of her future. Maybe the old woman had said, 'I'll tell them how happy you and Bill were,' or had cried, remembering that other time, when she was not old, when she did not have cataracts in her eyes, when the nice young couple invited her across the road for a glass of stout or a cup of tea. Or maybe the old woman had forgotten almost everything and just shook and stared. Whatever took place was never known, but in the hotel where Bridget drank the gin-and-lime and bought the crisps she chattered with the owner and asked him for his card, saying that she would be coming back there with her husband for a dinner. The locality, she said, was lucky for her, and she felt she owed it a little recompense. Half an hour later, she was around a tree, the car up on its hind legs, like an animal, her face on the dashboard, askew, her eyes wide open.

Some workmen who had been tarring the road heard the screech of the crash, and ran from a little caravan where they were cooking supper. None of them knew her. Two stayed while the third went to a lodge of a big house to ask to use the telephone. The woman in the gate lodge was a bit strange and did not want to let them in, so they had to go up to the big house, and quite a long time passed before the ambulance and the guards came. But the consensus was that she had died on the spot. She was brought back to the local hospital, where a young nurse laid her out in white. The mourners who came the next day were surprised, even aghast, that her face was so beautifully smooth, without cuts or gashes. It was makeup, they claimed, perfect makeup, and what a scandalous thing to adorn a corpse.

Michael knelt beside her and roared intemperately, as she had once roared, leaving no one in doubt that he loved her passionately. At the grave he tried to talk to her, tried to stop them from lowering the coffin. He knew everything now; he knew her plight and was helpless to do anything about it. She had quite a large funeral, but beneath the prayers and the murmurs were the whispers of how drunk she had been when she got into that car. They said her face had been disfigured, but that some silly nurse had made her look presentable, had doctored the truth, sent her to her maker with this monstrous camouflage – some chit of a nurse, as dissolute as Bridget herself had been.

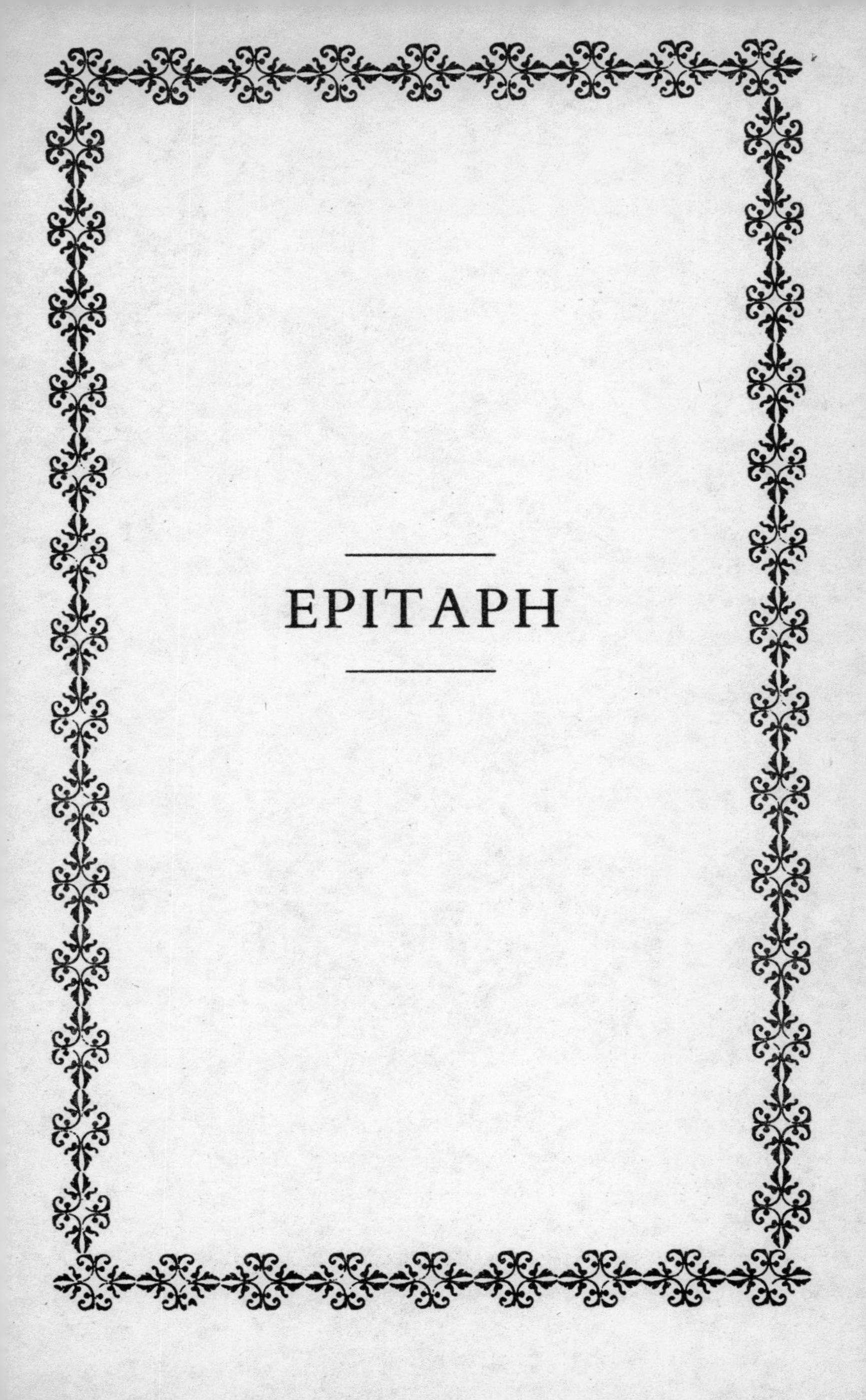

EPITAPH

When first i met you I thought it too good to be true. I was incredulous when I found that you, too, were smitten. You would ring me up and ask what I was wearing. You were espoused to satin and to velvet. Other times you would ring up and put the phone down, just to hear my voice. You probably thought it was a mere lark. One does think that, as a precaution. But you were lost and you knew it.

It was on a Greek island that I began to have some premonition of your slipping away from me. It was there I felt most permeated by you, even though you were absent. I hid. If people called, or threatened to call, I locked the door that led to the garden, and hence the house, and I lay on one of the straw mats and imagined I was holding you, hour after hour, cradling you, conversing, subject to the most eerie intimacy, as if you had come to rest in the roost of my mind, like a hen at night folded up in its own feathers. There were boats in the harbour, boats festooned with fairy lights and furled with flowers; there were dawns, blistering heat, golden evenings, a medley of stars, yet through them all I lay and basked and rocked back and forth to both the absence and the certainty of you.

When I returned to London, it was the ice zones. You looked so self-contained; like a cat, but with quick, close-to-flinching blue eyes that reminded me of aluminium before it is exposed to the weather. While I had been in Greece, you had been with your family in Arizona. You were going to be travelling, you said, first to one place, then another. You had never before discussed your travels. As you sat in my airy room, I asked myself a few predictably base questions. Even as you were making idle conversation about the low humidity in Arizona or the horse riding that had so relaxed you, I was imagining a little scenario. Perhaps on one of those languid evening rides you saw the woman you were married to in a new light, a little ahead of you on her horse, sauntering, in a dun corduroy outfit, her silhouette a representation of peace and maternity. You saw her and you were suddenly filled with a rekindling of your original love. Suddenly our love seemed too hectic, too feverish. I imagined that you gave yourself a bit of a talking-to, early one morning, by a canyon, and that maybe a friend was with you, a male friend, telling you to count your blessings, be thankful for what you had. A blast of sobriety took hold of you and God only knows how many resolutions you made. You had turned the corner. Life was going to be simple, wholesome. I laughed, and finding me laughing you cheered up somewhat, believing that I was not going to put my clutches on you. We kissed and embraced and so forth. Upon leaving, you had the audacity to warn me to be good.

When you left, I marched and marched about my room, uncontainable. I thought of a paddock from my childhood, a rectangular paddock with a stone wall around it. Some of the stones had been capsized, because horses were put in there for their daily bout of air – young wild unruly horses that would tramp and tramp, running from one corner to another, berserk, whinnying. This little paddock merely gave them the longing and the incentive to break loose, to get to the larger fields beyond. I saw the paddock and even the odd bit of flaking mortar that was put there to try to weld the loose stones together. I saw the hawthorn in blossom, pink and white lozenges on the spiky black branches. My own room, with its Prussian-blue walls, was like a tomb – a tomb that I wanted to break out of, except that I did not know how.

After that day, I don't know when I next saw you. It was months and months. You called on me, but you were curt, condescending. You had sprained your back and rather waspishly referred to swinging from chandeliers. I knew that a few bitter regrets had possessed you, because you looked racked. You were like those rich city cousins who come to the country one day a year and ask the locals so-called solicitous questions but are already tapping their watches to make sure not to miss the last train. Yet you were softening, showing some ardour, complimenting me. I must have responded too willingly, because all of a sudden you stepped back and announced that we would not be lovers any longer. You did not rule it out to the end of our days, but rule it out you did for the present and the foreseeable future. I felt an odd stab of pity at the way you could so readily restrain yourself. What were we now but ghosts in our lonely cerements? Yet I knew that it was not over, that another level had been reached, the underworld.

I had a dream of you. It must have been to do with your promotion, that 'poisoned chalice', as you called it, but I could see that you were gleeful about it. You had always felt some of your superiors to be hollow, and had no compunction about saying so. Fearless. On the crest. Unstoppable. You reminded me of a dead relative of mine, a man like you, upright, who ached to be a worldly hero even though his hidden nature was rather mystic.

In the dream you are going to be performing in a play and, as always, you are surrounded. It is in a quadrangle, and I am watching blind girls being led by a bigger blind girl. I have a word with her and she tells me about the play, and adds that she has put my name down to play one of the ghosts. Is it *Hamlet*, I wonder. I say to myself that inevitably I will be there as a ghost. Then you all file in, you and your entourage, and I run up to a gallery to hide, so as not to embarrass you. It is both church and theatre. There are banners, torches and a beautiful golden hanging lamp to denote the presence of Christ in the tabernacle. Suddenly there is a clamour, an uproar, shouts of men fighting and scuffling, people saying 'No, no,' and presently a man is being dragged out and laid on the aisle. He is your enemy and has been pasting you. Soon he gets up and goes towards the altar, where you are presiding, and he and you have a confab. Perhaps you are trying to make your peace with him. Your eyes are all that I can see, because of your face being lowered. Your poor eyes, they register such strain, such concern, and they are brown rather than blue.

I rang you just before Christmas. That time when all sorts of sentiments well up. I had the mistaken idea that you might yield, that you might even call on me, and I saw you, oh what idiocy, carrying a branch of mistletoe. The phone call lasted no more than sixty seconds. You had to go.

Across London, celebrations were rife, and I was included in one or two of them, as, indeed, were you. I went to a party – more correct to say I hobbled to a party – and learned that you were at another party with your family, holding hands, eating mince pie, singing carols. I was the unlucky recipient of this information because one of the guests, an unctuous and meddlesome man, had just come from that party and told all and sundry that you were a lot more agreeable than he had imagined. You have, of course, the reputation of being ruthless and possessed of a vaulting ambition.

Later that night, very late, sodden with wine and grief, I looked through a telephone directory for your home number and was dialling it when I happened to be saved by my son, returning from yet another party. Although he did not mention that I was doing something for which I would be ashamed, he conveyed it by coming stealthily into the room and standing there and making some little conversation about a Christmas Eve when we took a holiday sleigh ride in the snow and sang and asked riddles and were regaled by starry air and the crispness of the dry snow smarting under the runners of the sleigh. Christmases are buggers.

I remember another Christmas altogether, when you and I talked on the telephone and you mentioned that your children were so excited with the prospect of presents and overseas visitors that you had to give them aspirin.

'We had to give them aspirin,' you said. 'We.' I honestly thought that, with your expertise, you could have come up with something more effective. Anyhow, the night I dialled half of your number was one of those nights that one gets through without knowing how. I call them dead nights, since there is no memory whatsoever of undressing or getting into bed, or drinking from a carafe of water, or dreaming, or howling, or anything.

On Boxing Day, my son drove me a hundred miles to a clairvoyant in Gloucestershire. There was a blinding snowstorm, and encased in his little black sports car I felt – indeed, welcomed the notion – that we might skitter off the road. It was not that I wanted us dead but, rather, I wanted to be taken to another realm. Anyhow, we were lucky, because whenever we skittered we were saved by a grass bank or a gate or a demesne wall. Each time we escaped disaster we ate a boiled sweet as a sort of celebration. The plan was that while I saw this woman who was somehow going to pull out my pain as deftly as the midwife lifts out the slippery child, my son was going to drive in search of some beauties whom he knew, and afterwards he would fetch me to their home and we would have tea and plum cake and cinnamon toast. Comfort. Bliss. Three daughters he knew, and each had something particular and engaging about her. One worked as a florist; one bought and sold Oriental carpets and was a wanderer; one had an infectious laugh that was sometimes like a jennet's and sometimes like a nanny goat's.

'We might even stay the night,' he said, having a twofold thought – one the pleasure of such an event and the other the glaring fact that we were taking our lives in our hands by being out at all. There was a certain bravura in the way he went with the skids, allowing the car, like a wilful animal, to pursue its own course and then patting the steering wheel when things settled down again. Madness. Madness.

The clairvoyant told me that you would have been scornful of my childish nature. By saying 'would have' she already put you in the past tense, a goner. She told me incidental things – something about a maypole, a bridesmaid's bouquet, and the name of an English town where I had never set foot. As it happened, the beauties were unable to receive us, having a house chock-a-block with friends and cousins from all over the country; even the nursery was full up. We had tea in the hotel in the market square. The lounge, as they called it, was quite crowded. Families with their relatives; some of them in wheelchairs, others quite listless. There was a huge oil painting on the wall depicting hunters togged in brown coats, their dogs beside them. I was able to stare at a pointer with long liver-coloured ears and two retrievers who by their gums and gnashed teeth showed their naked relish. The pointer had a cruel, flexed gaze in his eye. The prone, feathered birds scattered about were like the thoughts within my head.

That Christmas passed, and the next, and the next, and so on, for I don't know how many years. Someone told me that he saw you at a Midnight Mass in the country looking very handsome, whereas you yourself had told me you were going to the Canaries with your family to get some sun. One doesn't know whom to believe. It got to be that any mention of you sent me dashing to other latitudes.

I went to Romania to a spa that was also a hotel. Small bedrooms, each with a concrete terrace, adjoined other bedrooms and other terraces, where at the weekends Romanians drowned their sullenness by drinking well into the night. Not a yodel or a ballad or even a refrain. On Sunday, lumpen women sitting in the lobby looking out at a few low rose bushes. A young girl asked me if I would give her my walking shoes and was piqued to learn that I would not. She kept pestering me. Another young girl asked me to buy her a bottle of whiskey. It was for the doctor who had delivered her baby.

Starvation inside and out. I had such a disgust towards the food – minced meat of some kind, with cabbage and scarcely boiled eggs – and this, mark you, was hotel fare. God only knows what the poor wretches ate in their own kitchens.

Not a single smile except on a poster, and then it was fairly unconvincing – a buxom woman in a bolero with more a crease than a smile. One evening there was a gypsy orchestra in the dining room, and as each gypsy came and sawed Strauss from his violin he whispered a request for a cigarette or a drink. Their wives had stationed themselves at the end of the dining room, fearing perhaps that their men would be wooed by some foreign nymphomaniac.

Each morning I had an injection which was supposed to rejuvenate me. Yes, I had you in mind when I went there. The rest of the day one was left to one's own devices. I would walk through the grounds, past a tennis court to a little allotment, where I was lured by the sight of a few vegetables and one small clump of white-and-lilac phlox that had the most startling effect, like flowers despatched from the moon. There was a woman working there, tending the vegetables, but she always dashed into her little hut when I appeared, determined to avoid me. She had in all about a kilo of tomatoes that were changing from green to red, nuggets of edible amber. She also had a few zucchini lying limply on their stalks, and several ridges of potatoes. The cabbages had been cut off; only the stumps were left. Alongside, there were other allotments, and on Sundays their owners would come and sit between their bits of vegetation and have a sort of picnic. I don't know why, but I was drawn back there day after day. Her incarceration made my own seem ridiculous, yet love is a prison too, so the sages say.

On my last day but one, when I went there I offered the woman my blue folding umbrella. She looked at me through her thick-lensed glasses as if I were mad and then ran into her little hut and pushed the door to – a wooden door, the wood the colour of a donkey. I did something quite silly; I opened the umbrella and put it inside the fence on the cindered path. A picture of absurdity – a bright blue umbrella with little golliwogs on its perimeter.

There are those who either wittingly or unwittingly try to make me forget you, scrap you. For instance, at lunch yesterday a friend went to great lengths to describe a painting which she felt I ought to see. It depicted a woman, probably a personable woman, sitting and waiting for someone, while at the margin of the painting stands a man, a suitor, whom she cannot or does not notice. My friend tried to tell me in all good faith how I was wasting my life by waiting. We were in a restaurant; she and her husband were visiting London and had invited a few friends for lunch. She said that when she married him she did it only as a stopgap, until Mr Right came along. Now she loved him as if he were Mr Right, which he was. She was wearing pearls and knobbled pearl earrings and she had grey-blue eyes. A pearled light issued from her, and it was like looking into one of those paperweights that are filled with falling snow.

She was trying to jolt me. She pointed to the surroundings – the lacquered walls, the potted palms, the mélange of people – and she said, 'Look, they're out there, lots of them. Just grab one of them while there's still time.' I looked. There were all kinds of people – young families, lovers, not-so-young women with hats and sultry makeup, and Oriental waiters trying in vain to answer the several demands of the hungry lunch-time throngs. All I could say to her was that if I had to wait for you, which I had, then wait I would.

'Bullshit,' she said, but in a friendly way.

She tried to buoy me up by suggesting ways we could make money – the jewellery business, for instance, or a wine bar. That was another thing. I have been improvident in waiting for you, buying fal-lals and all that, even buying a watercolour that I thought you would like. A doorway in Venice suspended above the canal.

'I want you to be happy,' she said. Her husband ate quickly and then she wanted him to eat the remainder of her lunch. He refused. She kept begging him and proffering forkfuls of mashed Dover sole.

'Please,' he said, and blushed like an altar boy. She kept

insisting. I thought he was going to leave.

You see, everyone is holding on. Just. If their skins were peeled off, or their chest bones opened, they would literally burst apart.

Of course I heeded what the woman in the restaurant had said. I began to ask myself why I waited. I thought that maybe it was something to do with my ancestors, one female ancestor in particular, some kind of expiation towards her. Are you like that? You once mentioned to me that you admired some Turkish warrior who achieved renown before he was thirty, but that was when you were young, bombastic.

She was a Bridget. An aunt. In my supplication I'm a bit like her. She wore knitted things, even knitted stockings, and I think she possessed one Sunday coat throughout her whole life. She was a widow at thirty, her husband having been shot by the Black and Tans. To make matters worse, her husband was partly on the side of the foe, since he worked for the constabulary and was something of a scab. Things get very twisted in this world, don't they; nothing is clear-cut. There he was blown to bits by the foe and yet not a hero, not a man for whom a ballad would be made up, or whose tragic fate would be an inspiration for other young men. Bitter. Bitter. She didn't have a little row of medals on a cloth tab to show to her son, or a letter from a dignitary to put in a frame. Anyhow, she carried on, saved the hay, fed the suckling calves, milked, churned, and was even so good-tempered as to make beautiful patterns out of the butter and to adorn the surfaces with little peaks, a tour de force. Each night, after reciting the rosary, she spoke tenderly – nay, erotically – to her dead husband. She cared for her son, brushed the nap of his fawn coat to make it smooth again, saved the leather buttons that fell off a sleeve for a future emergency, made jam, plum and greengage, the latter being a great novelty.

Food was her little indulgence, her sin. Each night, after the rosary and the paeans to her beloved, she made hot milk, to which she added sugar, and then she dunked bits of loaf bread in the milk and sucked and sucked as if she were sucking the bread of life. When she retired to bed she carried her china chamberpot up the stairs, and went to sleep and dreamed no doubt of things bad and good: her kine, the pet names she had given them, and the one tree of greengages – the green, she once envisaged, like globes clinging to an oval stone.

Other women complained of hallucinations or pulled down their bloomers on the chapel road, but not her; she kept toiling and moiling, she crooned, she forked the steaming manure onto the heap and with buckets of rain-water washed out the mangers. When her son went to college, she wept, wrote the weekly letter, and at Halloween sent a parcel containing apples, nuts and her speciality, porter cake. She fretted over how to pay the fees and paid them somehow, in fits and starts. Then catastrophe struck. Her animals contracted foot-and-mouth disease and died, their legs buckling under them, slobber oozing from their mouths. Neighbours rallied with jugs of milk and a flitch of pork or bacon when they killed a pig, but to her what was worst of all was the deserted farmyard – not even a goose or a little pullet to keep her company, nothing but empty outbuildings, a hay shed gapingly empty, a dairy smelling of disinfectant, the church idle, a silence that grated on her second by second.

But joy comes to all. Joy came to her when years later her son decided to come home from England and bring back his bride. It was as if she herself were embarking on marriage as she prepared for the great event. She made a straw hat and decked it with clusters of artificial violets, dusted over with a haze of white, making them look like real violets that had just had their first coat of frost. God knows where she got them. At the wedding she drank sherry and in a high quavering soprano voice sang 'My Cottage Home By Lough Sheelin's Side'. Not the most suitable song for a joyous occasion – a dirge, really – but the guests, or at least some of them, were as happy to cry as to laugh. They swallowed their tears with the same relish as the thin beef-tea soup. It was not a Type A breakfast; more a Type D or E.

Her son's bride – an Emily, no less – proved to be moody, and insisted that she and her husband sit in the parlour alone after supper while Mother-in-Law commanded the kitchen. A dead husband had been a different matter. Vaults do not open. Graves do not burst their seams of clay and yield up a moving hand or a shinbone or even a gaze. To have a son, a darling son, on the other side of the varnished door, in her very own abode, and not to be able to speak to him or hand him a mug of tea or consult him about next day's weather was a cross that she felt she could not bear.

Eventually she would crawl up to bed and cry, through the bolster into the very ticking. More than once in the night she would get up and hold the chamberpot aslant so in the next room they would not be mindful of her indiscretion, because to her all bodily functions were an indiscretion. She heard raised voices most nights from that next room, and their unhappiness hurt her far more than their happiness could ever have. She thought that maybe she should intervene, and occasionally she murmured about the suitability of her own death, but had to admit to herself that she was not ready for it. Devout she may have been and stainless in soul, but she feared death. Who doesn't? Don't I? Don't you?

So the poor woman listened night after night to the voices of the newlyweds and pondered. Sometimes she heard a door slam as if one or the other was on the point of leaving, and sometimes she heard silence, the sullen silence of two people awake but too proud to solicit forgiveness. Then again she heard tender voices, the meshing of limbs, the mew of the woman and the savage yodel of the man who in daylight was her mild son.

One rainy morning her son asked her if he could talk to her and he gestured to the front door.

'Mother of Jesus, he is going to evict me,' she said to herself as she followed, trying to gauge from the gait of his long spattered trenchcoat what his mood was. The hem of his coat was hanging, and she felt ashamed that she had not stitched it. They went to the hay shed, to be out of the rain, and as he leaned against the haystack he rolled a cigarette and said nothing. No melting words about parting being such sweet sorrow.

'Mother,' he said, and it was the very same as if her own dead mother had called her name and were about to rebuke her for having stolen a bun or only half milked a cow.

'Mother,' he said again.

'John,' she said, the tears welling up. Where would she go? She would have to live in a potato pit or take a room with some lonely neighbour.

'Emily's upset,' he said.

'Oh,' she said, as if that were something that just could not be countenanced. 'Is there anything I can do to help?'

Leaping to this friendly cue, he proceeded to tell her how insecure Emily felt, how banished, how it was no joke for Emily to leave Birmingham and bury herself in a mountainous swamp, in a bog. Worst of all, Emily felt herself to be an interloper, a mere lodger in the house where she ought to be mistress. Much more was said concerning Emily's early life, her difficult boozing father, the sudden death by drowning of one of Emily's sisters.

She had already in her mind given them the whole place,

lock, stock and barrel, and that night, when they had a friendly drink around the blazing fire, it was she who was the interloper in her own home. Though they drank each other's health with homemade elder wine, she must have had some intimation that the next equinox she would be going down the road carrying a bag, two baskets and an oil lamp.

She took lodgings in a house in a village nine miles away – a house with mildewed walls, so damp it was like a lime kiln; her fingers became like crooks, ludicrous prongs doubled over in prayer and still more prayer, as if her suffering were going to be efficacious, which it was not.

There came a day – don't ask me when – that you returned. Quite by surprise. You were a bit wound up. You had had an argument with the powers that be over your position and you were full of combat. You ate all before you. Olives, salami, taramasalata. The fact that you were not eating bread gave you reason to suppose that you could eat everything else to excess.

'Always more,' you said ruefully, like a little boy, as you dunked a soup-spoon of taramasalata onto a blade of chicory, then five or six more discs of Hungarian salami. It was sliced very thin, the specks of fat in it like crushed seed pearl. Then it was time to nestle, to come together. We had such a way with one another, so tender, like neighbouring icicles melting. But time had run out, your morning's argument had kept you longer than you meant, and now you were due back at work, bells were summoning you, inner bells and outer ones. I was sitting, as it happened, on the top step of the staircase, on that short piece that joined two landings. It was high summer. We had a habit of moving about a lot, some sort of ruse so as not to oppress one another. You came out in your light-blue summer suit and you said, 'Do you want me to take you on the stairs?'

'Yes,' I said, simulating a brazenness, and you thought about it and decided that the time was too short and announced that you would come back on the morrow. I stayed in the same place, on the top step of that short flight of stairs, facing an opaque window that had a border of red stained glass, in which there were little birds and crescents, like jellies inside two spheres of liquid red. You never allowed me to see you out, lest we be spotted, lest you be compromised. Sometimes it rankled and sometimes it didn't.

I raised the window up until the bottom half was level with the top, and through the lower space I looked out at summer, the tired sun-struck breathless air, the plane tree with both its foliage and its bobbins. I imagined biting on one of them, cracking the shell to get to the inner flesh, to get to the source, breaking my eyeteeth. Yes, there are times when we are not that far from the jungle. To calm myself I thought of something beautiful, virginal, and it was the white icing on a Christmas cake, a vast castellation, and I thought of the mother who fashioned it with her damp spatula, working on it to create valleys, peaks, a pinnacle to be gazed at, so beautiful that it cried out not to be eaten, and I wished that I had known you then. Ah yes, that was the rub of it – that we were children together from the beginning, the very beginning, and for all eternity.

You had left your tie. It sprawled over the back of the chair, resting on my white cardigan, two uneven tongues of blue spattered with black spots, and I looked at it with such conviction, as if you had just gone upstairs and were soon to come down again, discussing what we might do for dinner. I heard you. I did. I heard your footsteps. I thought maybe you had hidden or come in through the skylight, the way some lovers do to surprise the beloved. It was as bad as that.

Do you recall the time I met you on a train by chance about a year later? You were with your children. You all ate heartily; you ate fried eggs and bacon and chips and washed it all down with plastic cups of coffee. Then you used the little plastic stirrer to pick your teeth as you pointed knowingly to a big house on a hill or a motorbike track or an oncoming train. Naturally we would not be staying together when we got to the destination, so I asked if there was a walk, a bracing walk where I could get rid of the city cobwebs. You warmed to this. You drew me a little picture. You said I was to take the ferry; I was to cross over to the next county, and on arrival I would come upon a beautiful domain which was open to the public. Your children sensed how interested in me you were because of your drawing the picture, because of your saying, 'I'd be interested to know how you get on.'

I took the ferry next day. It was pouring with rain and there was a lashing wind. When I landed there was a tea shop cum antique shop, and I saw a little something that I yearned to give you. It was a ship within a bottle – an ivory ship encased in this bottle that seemed to have been rinsed in Reckitt's blue. The shop was closed. I went up the garden path through the turnstiles and into the public gardens along with all the other tourists. The rain had ceased, but it was shivering cold. The daffodils were out, two kinds – the very yellow ones that look like butter and the whitish ones like milk. Their petals were pitiful. Children were running in all directions, imagining this was their private garden, and grownups would stop in front of something to voice their admiration.

I felt a pang when I came on the house. A big house, majestic in its design. I recall it as being pink, but that may be a misconception. By pink I merely mean warm – a welcome, a glow. I fancied that you were up there waiting to receive me, while in fact I knew that you were elsewhere, with your children. They must have been surprised by your behaviour on the train, by your largesse. You threw money at them to go and get more eats. You were liberality itself. Showing both them and me how chivalrous you could be. A knight.

Another season altogether. Mellow ripeness, et cetera. The chestnuts shiny as an admiral's boots, their undersides a wandering creamy colour. It was just coming up to Remembrance Day. I snatched the poppy from the lapel of your tweed coat and looked at it, its crinolined edges and its functional wire stalk, and then I put it on my mantel.

'You will have to get another,' I said.

'I'm afraid I still love you,' you said almost balefully, as if you were having to say it in front of a whole class.

'In your heart of hearts?' I asked, and you nodded. I don't remember much else. We were sad and utterly understanding, the way people are in such situations. Ours was a small tragedy in comparison with the big ones, the world gone off the rails, righteous chants of madmen, rapine, pillage; ordinary mortals, feeling as insignificant as gnats. When you were leaving, you embraced me and you said, 'A lot has been said, a lot has been said.' We left it at that.

Atrocious solitudes. Supermarkets on Sunday, each customer with his or her own purchase – a pack of strong brown ale, a twisting vermilion sausage, like a snake, two pork chops under cellophane. I went to get a stamp to send you a valentine. They didn't sell stamps. 'Maybe you would have one in the till,' I said to the girl.

'I said we don't sell stamps,' she said. Pinched. Shrewish. White as an albino. No thought at all for anyone's plight. You wouldn't be taking her for a stroll down by the Salley Gardens. Do you ever take fancies to girls in shops?

That time I met you in a friend's apartment was very odd, very unsettling. I got there before you. I brought big bunches of summer flowers – stock and sweet William, things like that. When I arrived, there was such a smell of cats and cat pee that I shot to the three windows and opened them – so much so that the curtains, not snowy white, mark you, billowed into the room as if it were some theatre or opera house. Yet neither the breeze nor the flowers did anything to abate the horrible pong of cats. I imagined you noticing as you came through the door and thinking what Bolshie friends I had.

I agreed to meet you there because I had a team of builders refacing the outside of my crumbling house. For months I could not look out of the window without seeing a trouser leg or a face or a spattered overall, and I thought of you having to come there and feel compromised or spied upon. Anyhow I did not risk it. You came to the strange address. For once, you showed a bit of deference; in short, you did not comment on the smell or ask if there was someone in the other room. We talked politely, and then, at one moment, fearing that I was going to get up and go to you, to embrace you or something, you put your hand out and said, 'Sit, stay sitting!' As if I would embrace you, not having done so for many a year. Yet when you were leaving we did cling to one another like two dying creatures – dying of what?

Still, I was glad that you were leaving. It is not that one cannot bear the parting; it is really that one cannot bear the meeting, because of so many constraints. I kept trying to form a picture of you in the armchair in which you sat, as a keepsake. You had your legs stretched forward and you were somehow defenceless, like a warrior home from battle who has thrown all his armour at his feet. I could feel my heart going pitapat, pitapat while I was making so-called sensible conversation. I was going away. Far away. I was busy telling you, and myself, what a good thing it was, a golden opportunity. You took down numbers, the various numbers where I would be. It was understood that we might meet in that other country. Might. You were dashing off to buy a wedding present for someone who was going overseas to marry. I suggested a print, a print of Big Ben or the Thames or something historic. Meanwhile, I had that picture of you in my mind, my secret Odysseus returned from his wandering, reunited with his wife, his retinue, his dog. We said goodbye, three or four or five times; we clung; we fumbled for words, then parted. To think that it happened as cleanly as that.

there taking you and myself, after a conference [illegible] [illegible] Vincent [illegible] [illegible] [illegible] I would be. It [illegible] [illegible] that [illegible] [illegible] [illegible] [illegible] [illegible] [illegible] [illegible] off to buy a wedding present for [illegible] [illegible] [illegible] [illegible] many I [illegible] a [illegible] [illegible] [illegible] [illegible] [illegible] [illegible] [illegible] [illegible] [illegible] [illegible] that [illegible] of you [illegible]

WHAT A SKY

THE CLOUDS – DARK, MASSED AND PURPOSEFUL – raced across the sky. At one moment a gap appeared, a vault of blue so deep it looked like a cavity into which one could vanish, but soon the clouds swept across it like trailing curtains, removing it from sight. There were showers on and off – heavy showers – and in some fields the water had lodged in shallow pools where the cows stood impassively, gaping. The crows were incorrigible. Being inside the car, she could not actually hear their cawing, but she knew it very well and remembered how long ago she used to listen and try to decipher whether it denoted death or something more blithe.

As she mounted the granite steps of the nursing home, her face, of its own accord, folded into a false, obedient smile. A few old people sat in the hall, one woman praying on her big black horn rosary beads and a man staring listlessly through the long rain-splashed window, muttering, as if by his mutters he could will a visitor, or maybe the priest, to give him the last rites. One of the women tells her that her father has been looking forward to her visit and that he has come to the front door several times. This makes her quake, and she digs her fingernails into her palms for fortitude. As she crosses the threshold of his little bedroom, the first question he fires at her is 'What kept you?', and very politely she explains that the car ordered to fetch her from her hotel was a little late in arriving.

'I was expecting you two hours ago,' he says. His mood is foul and his hair is standing on end, tufts of grey hair sprouting like Lucifer's.

'How are you?' she says.

He tells her that he is terrible and complains of a pain in the back from the shoulder down, a pain like the stab of a knife. She asks if it is rheumatism. He says how would he know, but whatever it is, it is shocking, and to emphasize his discomfort he opens his mouth and lets out a groan. The first few minutes are taken up with showing him the presents that she has brought, but he is too disgruntled to appreciate them. She coaxes him to try on the pullover, but he won't. Suddenly he gets out of bed and goes to the lavatory. The lavatory adjoins the bedroom; it is merely a cupboard with fittings and fixtures. She sits in the overheated bedroom listening, while trying not to listen. She stares out of the opened window; the view is of a swamp, while above, in a pale untrammelled bit of whey-coloured sky, the crows are flying at different altitudes and cawing mercilessly. They are so jet they look silken, and listening to them, while trying not to listen to her father, she thinks that if he closes the lavatory door perhaps all will not be so awful; but he will not close the lavatory door and he will not apologize. He comes out with his pajamas streeling around his legs, his walk impaired as he goes towards the bed, across which his lunch tray has been slung. His legs like candles, white and spindly, foreshadow her own old age, and she wonders with a shudder if she will end up in a place like this.

'Wash your hands, Dad,' she says as he strips the bed-covers back. There is a second's balk as he looks at her, and the look has the dehumanized rage of a trapped animal, but for some reason he concedes and crosses to the little basin and gives his hands, or rather his right hand, a cursory splash. He dries it by laying the hand on the towel that hangs at the side of the basin. It is a towel that she recognizes from home – dark blue with orange splashes. Even this simple recollection pierces: she can smell the towel, she can remember it drying on top of the range, she can feel it without touching it. The towel, like every other item in that embattled house, has got inside her brain and remained there like furniture inside a room. The white cyclamen that she has brought is staring at her, the flowers like butterflies and the tiny buds like pencil tips, and it is this she obliges herself to see in order to generate a little cheerfulness.

'I spent Christmas Day all by myself.'

'No, Dad, you didn't,' she says, and reminds him that a relative came and took him out to lunch.

'I tell you, I spent Christmas Day all by myself,' he says, and now it is her turn to bristle.

'You were with Agatha. Remember?' she says.

'What do you know about it?' he says, staring at her, and she looks away, blaming herself for having lost control. He follows her with those eyes, then raises his hands up like a supplicant. One hand is raw and red. 'Eczema,' he says almost proudly. The other hand is knobbly, the fingers bunched together in a stump. He says he got that affliction from foddering cattle winter after winter. Then he tells her to go to the wardrobe. There are three dark suits, some tweed jackets, and a hideous light-blue gabardine that a young nun made him buy before he went on holiday to a convent in New Mexico. He praises this young nun, Sister Declan, praises her good humour, her buoyant spirit, her generosity and her innate sense of sacrifice. As a young girl, it seems, this young nun preferred to sit in the kitchen with her father, devising possible hurley games, or discussing hurley games that had been, instead of gallivanting with boys. He mentions how the nun's father died suddenly, choked to death while having his tea, but he shows no sign of pity or shock, and she thinks that in some crevice of his scalding mind he believes the nun has adopted him, which perhaps she has. The young nun has recently been sent away to the same convent in New Mexico, and the daughter thinks that perhaps it was punishment, perhaps she was getting too fond of this lonely, irascible man. No knowing.

'A great girl, the best friend I ever had,' he says. Wedged among the suits in the cupboard is the dark frieze coat that belongs to the bygone days, to his youth. Were she to put her hand in a pocket, she might find an old penny or a stone that he had picked up on his walks, the long walks he took to stamp out his ire. He says to look in the beige suitcase, which she does. It is already packed with belongings, summer things, and gallantly he announces that he intends to visit the young nun again, to make the journey across the sea, telling how he will probably arrive in the middle of the night, as he did before, and Sister Declan and a few of the others will be waiting inside the convent gate to give him a regal welcome.

'I may not even come back,' he says boastfully. On the top shelf of the wardrobe are various pairs of socks, and handkerchiefs – new handkerchiefs and torn ones – empty whiskey bottles, and two large framed photographs. He tells her to hand down one of those photographs, and for the millionth time she looks at the likeness of his mother and father. His mother seems formidable, with a topknot of curls, and white laced bodice that even in the faded photograph looks like armour. His father, who is seated, looks meeker and more compliant.

'Seven years of age when I lost my mother and father, within a month of each other,' he says, and his voice is now like gravel. He grits his teeth.

What would they have made of him, his daughter wonders. Would their love have tamed him? Would he be different? Would she herself be different?

'Was it very hard?' she asks, but without real tenderness.

'Hard? What are you talking about?' he says. 'To be brought out into a yard and put in a pony and trap and dumped on relations?'

She knows that were she to really feel for him she would enquire about the trap, the cushion he sat on, if there was a rug for his knees, what kind of coat he wore, and the colour of his hair then; but she does not ask these things. 'Did they beat you?' she asks, as a form of conciliation.

'You were beaten if you deserved it,' he says, and goes on to talk about their rancour and how he survived it, how he developed his independence, how he found excitement and sport in horses and was a legend even as a young lad for being able to break any horse. He remembers his boarding school and how he hated it, then his gadding days, then when still young – too young, he adds – meeting his future wife, and his daughter knows that soon he will cry, and talk of his dead wife and the marble tombstone that he erected to her memory, and that he will tell how much it cost and how much the hospital bill was, and how he never left her, or any one of the family, short of money for furniture or food. His voice is passing through me, the daughter thinks, as is his stare and his need and the upright sprouts of steel-coloured hair and the over-pink plates of false teeth in a glass beer tumbler. She feels glued to the spot, feels as if she has lost her will and the use of her limbs, and thinks, This is how it has always been. Looking away to avoid his gaze, her eyes light on his slippers. They are made of felt, green and red felt; there are holes in them and she wishes that she had bought him a new pair. He says to hand him the brown envelope that is above the washbasin.

The envelope contains photographs of himself taken in New Mexico. In them, he has the air of a suitor, and the pose and look that he has assumed take at least thirty years off his age.

At that moment, one of the senior nuns comes in, welcomes her, offers her a cup of tea, and remarks on how well she looks. He says that no one looks as well as he does and proffers the photos. He recounts his visit to the States again – how the stewardesses were amazed at his age and his vitality, and how everyone danced attendance on him. The nun and the daughter exchange a look. They have a strategy. They have corresponded about it, the nun's last letter enclosing a greeting card from him, in which he begged his daughter to come. From its tone she deduced that he had changed, that he had become mollified; but he has not, he is the same, she thinks.

'Now talk to your father,' the nun says, then stands there, hands folded into her wide black sleeves, while the daughter says to her father, 'Why don't you eat in the dining room, Dad?'

'I don't want to eat in the dining room,' he says, like a corrected child. The nun reminds him that he is alone too much, that he cries too much, that if he mingled it would do him some good.

'They're ignorant, they're ignorant people,' he says of the other inmates.

'They can't all be ignorant,' both the nun and the daughter say at the same moment.

'I tell you, they're all ignorant!' he says, his eyes glaring.

'But you wouldn't be so lonely, Dad,' his daughter says, feeling a wave of pity for him.

'Who says I'm lonely?' he says roughly, sabotaging that pity, and he lists the number of friends he has, the motorcars he has access to, the bookmakers he knows, the horse trainers that he is on first names with, and the countless houses where he is welcome at any hour of day or night throughout the year.

To cheer him up, the nun rushes out and shouts to a little girl in the pantry across the way to bring the pot of tea now and the plate of biscuits. Watching the tea being poured, he insists the cup be so full that when the milk is added it slops over onto the saucer, but he does not notice, does not care.

'Thank you, thank you, Sister,' he says. He used not to say thank you and she wonders if perhaps Sister Declan had told him that courtesy was one way to win back the love of recalcitrant ones. He mashes the biscuits on his gums and then suddenly brightens as he remembers the night in the house of some neighbours when their dog attacked him. He had gone there to convalesce from shingles. He launches into a description of the dog, a German shepherd, and his own poor self coming down in the night to make a cup of tea, and this dog flying at him and his arm going up in self-defence, the dog mauling him, and the miracle that he was not eaten to death. He charts the three days of agony before he was brought to the hospital, the arm being set, being in a sling for two months, and the little electric saw that the county surgeon used to remove the plaster.

'My God, what I had to suffer!' he says. The nun has already left, whispering some excuse.

'Poor Dad,' his daughter says. She is determined to be nice, admitting how wretched his life is, always has been.

'You have no idea,' he says, as he contrasts his present abode, a dungeon, with his own lovely limestone house that is going to ruin. He recalls his fifty-odd years in that house – the comforts, the blazing fire, the mutton dinners followed by rice pudding that his wife served. She reminds him that the house belongs to his son now and then she flinches, remembering that between them, also, there is a breach.

'He's no bloody good,' he says, and prefers instead to linger on his incarceration here.

'No mutton here; it's all beef,' he says.

'Don't they have any sheep?' she says, stupidly.

'It's no life for a father,' he says, and she realizes that he is about to ask for the guarantee that she cannot give.

She takes the tea tray and lays it on the hallway floor, then praises the kindness of nuns and of nurses and asks the name of the matron, so that she can give her a gift of money. He does not answer. In that terrible pause, as if on cue, one crow alights on a dip of barbed wire outside the window and lets out a series of hoarse exclamations. She is about to say it, about to spring the pleasant surprise. She has come to take him out for the day. That is her plan. The delay in her arrival at the nursing home was due to her calling at a luxurious hotel to ask if they did lunches late. When she got here from London, late the previous night, she had stayed in a more commercial hotel in the town, where she was kept awake most of the night by the noise of cattle. It was near an abattoir, and in the very early hours of the morning she could hear the cattle arriving, their bawling, their pitiful bawling, and then their various slippings and slobberings, and the shouts of the men who got them out of the trailers or the lorries and into the pens, and then other shouts, indeterminable shouts of men. She had lain in the very warm hotel room and allowed her mind to wander back to the time when her father bought and sold cattle, driving them on foot to the town, sometimes with the help of a simpleton, often failing to sell the beasts and having to drive them home again, with the subsequent wrangling and sparring over debts. She thinks that indeed he was not cut out for a life with cattle and foddering but that he was made for grander things, and it is with a rush of pleasure that she contemplates the surprise for him. She had already vetted the hotel, admitting, it is true, a minor disappointment that the service did not seem as august as the gardens or the imposing hallway with its massive portraits and beautiful staircase. When she visited to enquire about lunch, a rather vacant young boy said that no, they did not do lunches, but that possibly they could manage sandwiches, cheese or ham. Yet the atmosphere would exhilarate him, and sitting there in the nursing home with him now, she luxuriates in her own bit of private cheer. Has she not met someone, a man whose very voice, whose crisp manner fill her with verve and happiness? She barely knows him, but when he telephoned and imagined her surrounded by motley admirers, she did not disabuse him of his fantasy. She recalls, not without mischief, how that very morning in the market town she bought embroidered pillowcases and linen sheets, in anticipation of the day or the night when he would cross her bedroom doorway. The thought of this future tryst softens her towards the old man, her father, and for a moment the two men revolve in her thoughts like two halves of a slow-moving apparition. As for the new one, she knows why she bought pillowslips and costly sheets: because she wants her surroundings not only to be beautiful for him but to carry the vestiges of her past, such sacred things as flowers and linen, and all of a sudden, with unnerving clarity, she fears that she wants this new man to partake of her whole past – to know it in all its pain and permutations.

The moment has come to announce the treat, to encourage her father to get up and dress, to lead him down the hallway, holding his arm protectively so that the others will see that he is cherished, then to humour him in the car, to ply him with cigarettes, and to find in the hotel the snuggest little sitting room – in short, to give him a sense of well-being, to while away a few hours. It will be a talking point with him for weeks to come, instead of the eczema or the broken arm. Something is impeding her. She wants to do it, indeed she will do it, but she keeps delaying. She tries to examine what it is that is making her stall. Is it the physical act of helping him to dress, because he will, of course, insist on being helped? No, a nun will do that. Is it the thought of his being happy that bothers her? No, it is not that; she wants with all her heart to see him happy. Is it the fear of the service in the hotel being a disappointment, sandwiches being a letdown when he would have preferred soup and a meat course? No, it is not that, since, after all, the service is not her responsibility. What she dreads is the intimacy, being with him at all. She foresees that something awful will occur. He will break down and beg her to show him the love that he knows she is withholding; then, seeing that she cannot, will not, yield, he will grow furious, they will both grow furious, there will be the most terrible showdown, a slanging match of words, curses, buried grievances, maybe even blows. Yes, she will do it in a few minutes; she will clap her hands, jump up off the chair, and in a sing-song voice say, 'We're late, we're late, for a very important date.' She is rehearsing it, even envisaging the awkward smile that will come over his face, the melting, and his saying, 'Are you sure you can afford it, darling?', while at the same moment ordering her to open the wardrobe and choose his suit.

Each time she moves in her chair to do it, something awful gets between her and the nice gesture. It is like a phobia, like someone too terrified to enter the water but standing at its edge. Yet she knows that if she were to succumb, it would not only be an afternoon's respite for him, it would be for her some enormous leap. Her heart has been hardening now for some time, and when moved to pity by something she can no longer show her feelings –

all her feelings are for the privacy of her bedroom. Her heart is becoming a stone, but this gesture, this reach will soften her again and make her, if not the doting child, at least the eager young girl who brought home school reports or trophies that she had won, craving to be praised by him, this young girl who only recited the verses of 'Fontenoy' in place of singing a song. He had repeatedly told her that she could not sing, that she was tone-deaf.

Outside, the clouds have begun to mass for another downpour, and she realizes that there are tears in her eyes. She bends down, pretending to tie her shoe, because she does not want him to see these tears. She saw that it was perverse not to let him partake of this crumb of emotion, but also saw that nothing would be helped by it. He did not know her; he couldn't – his own life tore at him like a mad dog. Why isn't she stirring herself? Soon she will. He is talking non-stop, animated now by the saga of his passport and how he had to get it in such a hurry for his trip to America. He tells her to fetch it from the drawer, and she does. It is very new, with only one official entry, and that in itself conveys to her more than his words ever could: the paucity and barrenness of his life. He tells how the day he got that passport was the jolliest day he ever spent, how he had to go to Dublin to get it, how the nuns tut-tutted, said nobody could get a passport in that length of time because of all the red tape, but how he guaranteed that he would. He describes the wet day, one of the wettest days ever, how Biddy the hackney driver didn't even want to set out, said they would be marooned, and how he told her to stop flapping and get her coat on. He relives the drive, the very early morning, the floods, the fallen boughs, and Biddy and himself on the rocky road to Dublin, smoking fags and singing, Biddy all the while teasing him, saying that it is not a passport that he is going for but a mistress, a rendezvous.

'So you got the passport immediately,' the daughter says, to ingratiate herself.

'Straightaway. I had the influence – I told the nuns here to ring the Dáil, to ring my TD, and by God, they did.'

She asks the name of the TD, but he has no interest in telling that, goes on to say how in the passport office a cheeky young girl asked why he was going to the States, and how he told her he was going there to dig for gold. He is now warming to his tale, and she hears again about the air journey, the nice stewardesses, the two meals that came on a little plastic tray, and about how when he stepped out he saw his name on a big placard, and later, inside the convent gate, nuns waiting to receive him.

Suddenly she knows that she cannot take him out; perhaps she will do it on the morrow, but she cannot do it now; and so she makes to rise in her chair.

He senses it, his eyes now hard like granite. 'You're not leaving?' he says.

'I have to; the driver could only wait the hour,' she says feebly.

He gets out of bed, says he will at least see her to the front door, but she persuades him not to. He stares at her as if he is reading her mind, as if he knows the generous impulse that she has defected on. In that moment she dislikes herself even more than she has ever disliked him. Tomorrow she will indeed visit, before leaving, and they will patch it up, but she knows that she has missed something, something incalculable, a moment of grace. The downpour has stopped and the sky, drained of cloud, is like an immense grey sieve, sieving a greater greyness. As she rises to leave, she feels that her heart is in shreds, all over the room. She has left it in his keeping, but he is wildly, helplessly looking for his own.

STORM

THE SUN GAVE TO THE BARE FIELDS the lustre of ripened hay. That is why people go, for the sun and the scenery – ranges of mountains, their peaks sparkling, an almost cloudless sky, the sea a variety of shades of blue, ceaselessly flickering like a tray of jewels. Yet Eileen wants to go home; to be more precise, she wishes that she had never come. Her son Mark, and his girlfriend, Penny, have become strangers to her and, though they talk and go to the beach and go to dinner, there is between them a tautness. She sees her age and her separateness much more painfully here than when at home, and she is lost without the props of work and friends. She sees faults in Penny that she had not noticed before. She is irked that a girl of twenty can be so self-assured, irked at the languid painstaking way that Penny applies her suntan oil, making sure that it covers each inch of her body, then rolling onto her stomach imploring Mark to cover her back completely. At other times Penny is moody, her face buried in a large paperback book with a picture of a girl in a gauze bonnet on the cover. There are other things, too: when they go out to dinner Penny fiddles with the cutlery or the salt-and-pepper shakers, she is ridiculously squeamish about the food, and offers Mark tastes of things as if he were still a baby.

On the third night, Eileen cannot sleep. On impulse she gets out of bed, dons a cardigan and goes out on the terrace to plan a strategy. A mist has descended, a mist so thick and so opaque that she cannot see the pillars and has to move like a sleepwalker to make her way to the balustrade. Somewhere in this sphere of milky white the gulls are screaming, and their screams have a whiff of the supernatural because of her not being able to see their shapes. A few hours earlier, the heavens were a deep, a hushed blue, studded with stars; the place was enchanting, the night balmy and soft. In fact, Penny and Mark sat on the canvas chairs looking at the constellations while waiting and hoping for a falling star so that they could make a wish together. Eileen had sat a little apart from them, lamenting that she had never been that young or that carefree. Now, out on the terrace again, staring into the thicket of mist and unnerved by the screaming gulls, she makes herself a firm promise to go home. She invents a reason, that she has to do jury duty; then, like a sleepwalker, she gropes her way back to bed.

But next day she finds herself lying on the beach near them, smarting beneath a merciless sun. There is a little drama. Penny has lost a ring and Mark is digging for it in the sand. He scrapes and scrapes, as a child might, and then he gets a child's shovel which has been left behind and digs deep, deeper than is necessary. He retraces where he has already scraped. Penny is crying. It was a ring Mark gave her, an amethyst. Eileen would like to help, but he says he knows where he has already searched and it is best to leave it to him. Penny dangles her long, elegant fingers and recalls how the ring slipped off. He jokes a little and says what a pity that she hadn't called out at the very moment, because then they could trace it. Others watch, some supposing that it is money that is lost. Penny begs him to give up, saying that obviously it was meant and alluding to possible bad luck. He goes to a different spot.

'It can't be there,' Penny says, almost crisp. Eileen sees that he is smiling. She does not see him pick anything up, but soon after he stands over Penny, bends down and re-enacts the ritual of putting on an engagement ring. Penny cries out with joy and disbelief, says she can't believe it, and a great ripple of warmth and giddiness overtakes them. Mark is fluent now with stories of life at university, fights he got into, scrapes he got into, being stopped by the police on his motorcycle and so on, as if the relief of finding the ring has put to rest any unspoken difference between them.

In the late afternoon they drive back to the villa and discuss where they should go for dinner. Penny decides to cut her fringe and stations herself at the kitchen table wielding a huge pair of scissors, the only pair in the house, while Mark holds a small, shell-shaped mirror in front of her. Sometimes in jest Penny puts the point of the scissors to his temple or nips a little hair from above his ear and they joke as to who is the bigger coward. Afterwards, the shreds of cut blond hair lie on the table, but Penny makes no attempt to sweep them up. They have drinks and the bits of hair are still there, dry now and exquisitely blond. Eileen eventually sweeps them up, resenting it, even while she is doing it.

When they arrive for dinner they are bundled out onto a terrace and told they must wait.

'*Aspetta ... aspetta,*' the waiter keeps saying, although his meaning is already clear. Eileen notices everything with an awful clarity, as if a gauze has been stripped from her brain – the metal chairs glint like dentist's chairs, a pipe protruding from underneath the terrace is disgorging sewage into the sea, while a little mongrel dog barks at the sewage with untoward glee. The waiter brings three tall glasses filled with red Campari and soda.

'It's just like mouthwash,' Penny says, wiggling one of the straws between her lips. Eileen is doing everything to be pleasant, but inside she feels that she will erupt. First she counts backwards from one to a hundred, then she takes a sip from her glass, not using a straw, then resumes counting and wonders if they, too, are aware of the estrangement. She is meaning to tell them she will go home earlier than planned, but each time she is on the point of saying it, there is some distraction, Penny asking for a fresh straw, or the mongrel now at their table, or two people identically dressed and with similar haircuts, their gender a mystery.

As they drive back to the villa after dinner, it happens. Its suddenness is stunning. Eileen does not understand how it happens except that it does: a sharp word, then another, then another, then the eruption.

'Are you all right in the back?' he asks.

'Fine,' Eileen says.

'We're not going too fast for you?' he asks.

'If Penny were driving too fast I'd tell her to slow down.'

'Huh . . . it wouldn't make any difference,' Penny says. 'I'd tell you to hitch.' Eileen bristles. She infers in this insolence, dislike, audacity. Suddenly she is speaking rapidly, gracelessly, and she hears herself saying cruel things, mentioning their moodiness, cut hairs, the cost of the villa, the cost of the very car they are driving in, and even as she says this she is appalled. In contrast they are utterly still, and the only change she sees is Mark's hand laid over Penny's. Eventually Eileen becomes silent, her outburst spent, and they drive without saying a word. When they arrive home, they stagger out of the car and she sees them walk towards the villa with an air of exhaustion and defeat. She hurries, to try and salvage things.

'We must talk,' she says to Mark, and touches his sleeve. He flings her off as if she were vermin. It is his turn to explode. His rage is savage and she realizes that a boy who has been mild and gentle all his life is cursing her, vehemently. Penny clings to him as if he were a mast, begging him not to be angry, and there is such terrifying contrast between the tender appeal of her sobs and the rabidness of his words as he denounces his mother. She, too, looks at him, begging him to stop, and sees that the whites of his eyes are the colour of freshly shed blood. He has passed sentence on her forever. A thousand memories pass through her as she begs to be allowed to explain herself. He will not hear of it. When he finishes his exhortation, he leads Penny towards the open door and they go out, down the steps and up the path to the gateway. Eileen knows that to call after them is useless, and yet she does. They disappear from sight, and turning round in the kitchen, she does something that she knows to be absurd: she dons an apron and goes to the sink to wash the glasses that have been there since before they went out. She washes them in soapy water, rinses them under the hot tap, then under the cold tap, and dries them until they are so dry that she can hear the whoosh of the cloth on the dry glass.

Soon the kitchen is utterly silent. She can hear the lap of water through the open window and the clatter from the rigging of the few boats that bob back and forth in the breeze. She is waiting both for the sound of the car to start up or for their return. She combs her hair, walks around her bedroom, consults her bedside clock and listens for them. After an hour she undresses and turns out her light in the belief that the dark house and the knowledge that she has gone to bed will bring them back. Lying there, praying – a thing she has not done for years – she hears them come in on tiptoe, and without any premeditation she rushes out to the passage and in one burst apologizes and says some madness possessed her. Idiotically she mentions sunstroke, and they look at each other with blanched and mortified faces.

In the morning they all rise earlier than usual and she can see that, like her, they did not sleep. They are quiet; they are utterly thoughtful and polite, but they are embarrassed. She asks a favour of them. She reminds them that for days they had planned to go sailing and she wonders if they could go today, as she would welcome the day to herself. They are relieved and, as she can see, quite glad, and without even touching their breakfast they get up and start to gather a few things – towels, bathing suits, suntan oil and bottled water in case, as Mark says, they are marooned! She waves goodbye to them as they drive off. When they have gone she comes back into the house, makes another pot of tea and sits by the table, moping. Later she makes her bed and then closes the door of their bedroom, not daring, or wanting, to venture in. The floor of their room is strewn with clothes – a pink chiffon dress, silver shoes, a sun hat and, most wrenching of all, a threadbare teddy bear belonging to Penny.

Eileen gathers up the large bottles that had contained seltzer water and walks to the little local supermarket with them to collect a refund. She is carrying a dictionary in order to make the transaction easier. In the little harbour a few children are bathing and paddling while their mothers sit on large, brightly-coloured towels, talking loudly and occasionally yelling at the children. It is not a beach proper, just a harbour with a few fishing boats and a pathetically small strip of sand. After she has exchanged the bottles she comes and sits next to the local mothers, not understanding a word of what they are saying. Everywhere there are children: children darting into the water, children coming out and begging to be dried, children with plastic bubbles like eggs strapped to their backs to enable them to swim, children wet and slippery as eels, teeth chattering. Two small boys in red seersucker bathing suits are arguing over a piece of string, and as she follows the line of the string with her eyes she sees a kite, high above, fluttering in the air. The fine thread sustaining the kite suggests to her that thin thread between mother and child and it is as if the full meaning of motherhood has been revealed to her at last. Although not a swimmer, she decides to go in the water. She thinks that it will calm her, that her agitation is only caused by the heat. She rushes home to fetch a bathing suit and towel, and on the way there convinces herself that Mark and Penny have come back.

'Yoo-hoo,' she says as she enters the kitchen, and then goes towards their bedroom door and knocks cautiously. As there is no answer, she goes inside and starts to make their bed. She pulls the cover off in one rough gesture, pummels the mattress and then very slowly and patiently makes the bed, even folding back the top sheet the way it is done in hotels. She then picks up the various garments from the floor and starts to hang them in the already crammed closet. She notices that Mark has brought two dark suits, a cream suit, sports jackets and endless pairs of leather shoes. She wonders what kind of vacation he had envisioned and suddenly realizes that for them, too, the holiday must seem a fiasco. Her mood veers between shame and anger. They should have understood, should have apologized, should have been more sympathetic. She is alone, she has recently been jilted, she has dreamed of her lover on a swing with his wife, both of them moving through the air, charmed, assured creatures. Great copious tears run down her face onto her neck, and as they reach her breastbone she shivers. These tears blind her so that the red tiles of the floor appear to be curving, the roses on the bedspread float as if on a lake, and the beaded eyes of the teddy bear glint at her with malice. She will swim, or she will try to swim; she will dispel this frenzy.

At the harbour she lifts her dress off shyly, and then with considerable shame she reaches for her water wings. They are blue plastic and they carry a flagrant advertisement for a suntan lotion. Standing there in the water is a boy of about eighteen holding a football and letting out the most unseemly and guttural sounds. He is a simpleton. She can tell by the way he stares. She tries to ignore him, but sees the ball come towards her as she makes her intrepid passage through the water. The ball hits her shoulder, so she loses her balance, wobbles and takes a second to stand up straight again. The simpleton is staring at her and trying to speak, a foam of spittle on his lips. Drawing off her wings, she looks into the distance, pretending that she is not aware of him. He moves towards her, puts a hand out and tries in vain to catch hold of her, but she is too quick. She hurries out of the water, positions herself against a rock and cowers inside a huge brown fleecy towel. He follows. He is wearing a chain around his neck, attached to it a silver medal with a blue engraving of the Virgin Mary. His skin is mahogany colour. He comes close to her and is trying to say something or suggest something, and trembling inside the big brown towel, she tells him in his language to go away, to get lost. 'Vamoose,' she says, and flicks the back of her hand to confirm that she is serious. Then one of the local women yells abuse at him and he goes off silently into the water, tossing the ball to no one in particular.

At home, forcing herself to have lunch, Eileen begins to admit the gravity of things. She realizes now that Mark and Penny have left. She pictures them looking at a cheap room on some other part of the island, or perhaps buying a tent and deciding to sleep on the beach. On her plate colonies of ants are plundering the shreds of yellow and pink flesh that have adhered to a peach pit, and their assiduousness is so utter that she has to turn away.

She hurries out, takes a short cut across a field, through some scrubland to the little white church on the hill. It is like a beehive, and she thinks, as she goes toward it, that somehow her anguish will lessen once she gets inside, once she kneels down and prostrates herself before her Maker. The door is locked yet she tries turning the black iron knob in every direction. She walks around to find that the side door is also locked, and then, attempting to climb the pebble wall in order to look in the window, she loses her grip halfway and grazes her knee. She looks apologetically in case she has been seen, but there is no one there. There is simply a ragged rosemary bush and some broken bottles – the relics of a recent binge. She breaks off a few sprigs of rosemary to put in their bedroom.

'I am doing things as if they are coming back,' she says as she searches for wildflowers. Walking down from the chapel she is again assailed by the sight of children, children refreshed from their siestas, pedalling furiously on tricycles and bicycles, children on a rampage through the street, followed by a second gang with feathers in their hair, wielding bows and arrows. Mindlessly she walks, and her steps carry her away from the town towards a wood. It is a young wood and the pine trees have not grown to any reasonable height, but their smell is pleasant and so is the rustle of the russet needles. She listens from time to time for a chorus of birds but realizes that there are none and hears instead the distant sough of the sea. Some trees have withered, are merely grey, shorn stumps, dry and leafless. They remind her of her anger and once again she recalls last night's scene, that snapshot glued to her retina.

Three youths on motorcycles enter the wood and come bounding across as if intent on destroying themselves and every growing thing. They are like a warring clan, and they shout as they come towards her. She runs into a thicket and, crouching, hides under the trees out of their sight. She can hear them shouting and she thinks that they are calling to her, and now on hands and knees she starts to crawl through the underbrush and make her way by a hidden route back to the town. Scratches do not matter, nor does the fact that her clothing is ripped; her one concern is to get back among people, to escape their ravages and her escalating madness. It is while she is making her way back that the light changes and the young trees begin to sway, like pliant branches. A wind has risen and in the town itself the houses are no longer startling white but a dun colour, like houses robbed of their light. Dustbin lids are rolling along the street and not a child or an adult is in sight. All have gone indoors to avoid the storm. On the water itself boats are like baubles, defenceless against the brewing storm. On the terrace, the canvas chairs have fallen over, and so, too, has her little wooden clothes-horse with its tea towels. As she crosses to retrieve them the umbrella table keels forward and clouts her. Her mind can jump to only one conclusion – she sees Mark and Penny in a sailboat, Penny exclaiming, Mark jumping and tugging at the sails, trying in vain to steer them to safety. She does not know where Penny's parents live and at once runs to their bedroom to look for her passport. The beautiful childlike face that looks out at her from the passport photograph seems to be speaking to her, begging, asking for clemency. She sees them in the middle of the ocean, flung apart by the waves, like ill-starred lovers in a mythological tale. The next moment she tells herself that Mark is a capable sailor and will lead them to safety. Then she is asking aloud where she will bury them, forgetting that they are lost at sea.

'Nonsense . . . nonsense,' a voice that is her own shouts, insisting that islanders would not rent a sailing boat on such a day. She runs from room to room, closing doors and windows against a gale that rampages like a beast. Suddenly there is a knock, and putting on a semblance of composure, she runs to open the door, only to find that there is no one there. She stares out in the pitch-black and believes the keening wind to be a messenger of death.

The hours drag on, and in those hours she knows every shade of doubt, of rallying, of terror and eventually of despair. She remembers a million things, moments of her son's childhood, his wanting to pluck his long curved eyelashes and give them to her, a little painted xylophone he had had, stamps that he collected and displayed so beautifully under single folds of yellow transparent paper. She sees Penny tall and stalklike in her tight jeans and pink T-shirt with pearl droplets stitched to the front, her eyes flashing, dancing on his every whim.

At seven she sets out for a restaurant, believing that by doing so she will hasten their return. A note of optimism grips her. They will be back, and what is more, they will be famished. The restaurant is empty, so that she has a choice of tables. She chooses one near the window and looks out over the sea, which is no longer churning but is grey and scowling in the aftermath of the storm. In fact, she realizes that she cannot look at the sea, so she quickly changes tables. The owner and his daughter, who are laying out other tables, give each other a shrug. She is not welcome. For one thing, she has come too early and for another she is being stroppy about tables. She orders a bottle of the best wine. The daughter brings it with a dish of green olives. At moments, hearing footsteps, Eileen half rises to welcome Mark and Penny, but those who enter are other waiters arriving for work, removing jackets as they cross the floor. Soon the restaurant takes on a festive appearance. The daughter folds the napkins into shapes that look like fezzes and she carries them on a tray, along with vases each containing a single rose. The guitar music is much too harsh, and Eileen asks for it to be put lower, but her request is ignored. Yes, she does admit that Penny and Mark are thoughtless to have stayed out so long and not to be back for pre-dinner drinks, yet she will not scold them, she will make a big fuss over them. She has already asked if there is lobster and has asked for three portions to be put aside. 'But suppose they don't come,' she asks aloud, as if addressing another person. The daughter, who decidedly does not like her, hears this and mutters something to her father. Eileen now asks herself irrational questions, such as if they have not arrived by eight, or at the latest by eight thirty, should she eat, and if they do not arrive at all, will she be obliged to pay for the lobsters? She opens her purse and looks at the mauve-tinted cheques, flicking her finger along each one, wondering if she has enough money to defray the expenses that most certainly will be hers.

No sooner has she finished the first glass of wine than the tears start up and the owner, who until then has disliked her, comes over to the table to enquire what is the matter.

'*Morto*,' she says as she looks up at him, and now he becomes solicitous and asks her in broken English to explain to him what the matter is.

'*Il mare*,' she says, and he nods and describes the fury of the storm by puffing out his cheeks and making awesome gulping sounds. Upon hearing her story, he pushes away the wine bottle and tells his daughter, Aurora, to bring cognac. Eileen realizes that it must be grave indeed, because of his ordering the cognac. He recalls a drowning in their little village, the grief and horror, the darkness that descended, and although she cannot understand everything that he is saying, she gets the gist of it and wrings her hands in terror. He crosses to the counter and quickly dials the phone, all the time looking in her direction in case she does an injury to herself. Then as soon as the phone is picked up at the other end, he turns away and talks hurriedly, leaving her to assume the worst. He comes back proudly twirling his moustache and in halting English tells her that no news of a sailing accident has been reported to the lifeboat people.

'Courage, courage, courage,' he says, confident that the anguish will turn to laughter before long. By about nine she decides to go back to the house and he assures her that a table will be kept for the hungry ones. Then he dashes to the counter and takes from a jug two roses, which he gallantly gives her, along with his card.

The villa is dark, dark as a tomb, and she runs in and switches on all the lights.

'They'll come in the next five minutes,' she says, quite convinced, and even dares to stare up at the wall clock with its spider-like hands. They do not come. They will not come. The patron of the restaurant is her one friend. He will help her with the formalities, he will talk to the police for her, he will see to it that the divers go down. But what then? What then? she asks, her voice quivering. With each fresh admission she feels that the measure of her delirium is heaped full and that she cannot bear it, yet mind and body dart to the next awful minute. She walks all around the table touching its surface, then into the bathroom and out again, and back and around the table, and then into the two bedrooms, first her own, then theirs, and draws back the covers ceremoniously as if for a honeymoon couple. The clock and woodcuts on the wall are askew and she sets about straightening them. Then she commences a letter to the owner of the villa, who lives in Madrid, explaining why she has had to leave sooner than expected. By doing this she is admitting the worst. She is very calm now and her handwriting clear as a child's. She thinks of Penny's parents, whom she has never met, foresees their grief, their shock, their rage, their disbelief. How could they lose such a daughter, Penny, Penelope, the embodiment of cheer and sunniness? Her father, being an army man, will probably take it better, but what of her mother, the overweight woman whom Penny described as being psychic? Maybe she already knows, has seen her daughter in the depths of the ocean, among the preying fishes. Then, with a grief too awful to countenance, she sees Mark with the bloodshot eyes and recalls his renunciation of her.

There is a beam of headlights in her drive and immediately she rallies, concluding that it is the police, but as she rises she hears the small friendly hoot that is their signal. All of a sudden she feels ridiculous. They come in, bright, tousled and brimming with news. They tell how they met an Englishman with a metal detector who took them on a tour of the island, showed them old ruins and burial grounds, and how later they went to a hotel and swam in the pool but had to hide underwater each time a waiter went by. They are giddy with happiness.

'Did you sail?' she asks Mark.

'We did, but it got a bit dangerous,' Mark says, guessing how she must have panicked. Together he and Penny tell her of a beautiful restaurant where they have been; tables tucked away in corners, the cloths, the flowers, the music and above all, the scrumptious food – sweet mutton, zucchini and potatoes cooked with mint and butter.

'We're going to take you tomorrow night,' Penny says with a smile. It is the first time they have looked at each other since the outburst and Eileen now feels that she is the younger of the two and by far the more insecure. Penny has forgiven her, has forgotten it. The day has brought her closer to Mark and she is all agog.

'We've booked a table,' Mark says and wags a finger at Eileen to indicate that they are taking her, that it is to be their treat.

'I think I should go home,' she says, lamentably.

'Don't be silly,' he says and the look that he gives her is

full of both pity and dread. She is on the point of telling him about the day, the scrubland, the youths, the storm, her frenzy, but his eyes, now grave and moist, beg her not to. His eyes ask her to keep this pain, this alarm, to herself.

'What did you do?' he asks nevertheless.

'Oh, lots of jolly things,' she says, and the lie has for her, as well as for him, all the sweetness and freshness of truth. For the remainder of the vacation they will behave as if nothing has happened, but of course, something has. They have each looked into the abyss and drawn back, frightened of the primitive forces that lurk there.

'Tomorrow ...' he says and smiles his old smile.

'Tomorrow ...' she says, as if there was no storm, no rift, as if the sea outside was a cradle lulling the world to a sweet, guileless sleep.

ANOTHER TIME

IT HAPPENS TO ONE AND ALL. It is given many names, but those who have it know it for what it is – the canker that sets in and makes one crabbed, finding fault with things, complaining, full of secret and not-so-secret spleen. Nelly knew it. She knew she was in trouble after that dream. She dreamed that one of her children had stripped her of everything, even her teeth, and when she wakened she decided that it was time to get away. 'Get away, get away,' she said several times to herself as she hurried up the street to a travel agent's to look at brochures. In a small, unprepossessing office she saw posters of walled cities, all of which were gold-coloured; she saw churches, canals, castles; and each one filled her not with expectations but with doom. It was as bad as that. Suddenly it came to her. She would go home – not to her own people but to a small seaside town about twenty miles from there, a place she had always yearned to go to as a child, a resort where some of the richer people had cottages. It was remote and primitive, on the edge of the Atlantic, the white houses laid out like kerchiefs. She had seen photos of it, and it had for her a touch of mystery, a hidden magic; it was a place where people went when they were happy – newlyweds and those who got legacies. There was a jetty across, so although an island it was not cut off completely, and she was glad of that. The ocean could pound or lap on three sides and yet she had a link with the land, she could get away. Getting away preoccupied her, as if it would lead to redemption.

As she crossed the threshold of the bedroom in her hotel, she saw that it did not bode well. It was a tiny room, with a tiny sagging bed, bits and pieces of tasteless furniture, and a washbasin in one corner with a vein of rust running down from one of the taps. The coat hangers were of metal, and either they were buckled or their hooks were so attenuated that they looked like skewers. A view of the ocean, yes, but it was not an expanse, more a sliver of grey-green sulky sea.

It will be better, she thought, fearing that it wouldn't. She could hear the man in the next room as she hung her clothes. He was coughing. He's lonely, she thought, that's why he's coughing. After she had hung her clothes, she put on a bit of makeup before going down to have a drink with the owners. The owners had welcomed her and asked her to have an early drink before dinner. On impulse, she gave them the bottle of champagne that she had bought at the airport, and now she wished she hadn't. They seemed so taken aback by it – it was too patrician – and it was not chilled.

Opening the champagne took quite a while, because the husband was more interested in telling her about some of his more exotic travels than in wheedling the cork out. The wife was a bit heavy and had a sleepy, sad face with big spaniel eyes. They seemed to have no children, as children were not mentioned. The husband held forth about jobs he had held in Borneo or Karachi or wherever – that was when he was in oil. Then at length he had decided to settle down, and he found himself a wife, and they came back to Ireland, to their roots, and bought this hotel, which was something of a legend. The previous owner was an eccentric and made people do morris dancing and drink mead.

No morris dancing now, Nelly thought as they lifted their glasses. They were tiny glasses – sherry glasses, really – and the champagne was tepid. Just as the cork flew out, a tall boy had come in from the kitchen and stared. He was a simpleton – she could tell by his smile and the way he stared and then had to be told by the wife to go back in to mind the cabbage.

'Go in, Caimin,' she said.

'Yes, ma'am,' he said, coveting the green cork, with its dun-gold paper. The husband was telling Nelly that she had picked a most unfortunate evening for her first dinner. They were overbooked, jam-packed. A party of twelve at one table alone. He himself had not taken the booking; a silly young girl had taken it over the phone. He apologized in advance. Nelly looked around the dismal room, with its checked tablecloths and kitchen chairs, and was not regaled by what she saw. There were empty wine bottles above the sideboard and all along the wall ledge. They were green and dusty and served no purpose whatsoever, and she supposed that the champagne bottle would go up their somewhere and be just as useless. He wasn't pouring fast enough for her. She wanted to drink in great gulps, to forget her surroundings, to be removed from them, to forget the impulse for her coming, and to blot out the admission that she had made a mistake.

'We reserved you that table,' he said, pointing to a table in the corner, close to the window, with a view of the road outside. The road was covered with mist and the summer evening could easily pass for October or November. Suddenly radio music and loud voices came from the kitchen, and then a buxom girl emerged followed by another girl with long plaits. They had come to lay the tables. They were big, strapping girls, and they more or less slung the plates and the cruets onto the tables and made a great clatter with the cutlery box. They eyed Nelly sitting there with the boss and the Mrs, and one of them whispered something to the other – probably about her being a big shot, maybe even someone from the Tourist Board. Occasionally they would laugh, and the simpleton would rush from the kitchen, holding a ladle or a saucepan in his hand, to join in the levity. Soon the wife rose, put her hands to her chest, and said very formally, 'Duty calls.' Then the husband picked up the bottle of champagne and said, 'We'll chill the rest of this for you. You can have it with your meal.'

As she turned the key in her bedroom door, Nelly met her neighbour. He wore a suit and a cap, and it was clear that he was not accustomed to being on holiday. His first remark was how beautiful the hotel was – a palace. A palace! A bit of dark landing with linoleum and off-white doors, like hospital doors, leading to the rooms; a sickly maidenhair fern in a big brass jardiniere. He spoke with a clipped Northern accent as he enlarged on the glories of the place, the seashore where he had just been walking, the peace and quiet, and the big feeds. He was on his way to the public house for a few jars before dinner. Would she care to join him? She realized that he had been waiting to pounce, that he must have heard of her arrival – a woman on her own – and that he had assumed they would become friends. She declined. He asked again, thinking she said no only out of courtesy. She declined more firmly. She saw the smile leave his face. She saw the scowl. He could hardly endure this rebuff. His anger was rising. He pulled his key from his pocket and, for no reason, proceeded to open his door again. Anything to withhold his rage. They were from the same country, God damn it; just because she lived abroad was no reason to snub him. She could read his inner thoughts and guess his outrage by the obsequiousness of what he then said.

'Aah, thanks a lot,' he said, and repeated it twice over, when in fact he wanted to strike her. He had reverted to some shaming moment when he had thanked a superior whom he really hated.

I have made an enemy, she thought as she entered her room. She went straight to the washbasin and splashed her face fiercely with douches of cold water.

Dinner was indeed a boisterous affair. The party of twelve was mostly children, ranging from teenagers to a baby in a high chair. The mother addressed each child by name, over and over, sometimes admonishing, sometimes approving, so that Nelly soon knew that the baby was called Troy, short for Troilus, and would have to eat those mashed potatoes before he got his mashed banana. The mother was a strong, bossy woman, and without these hordes of children to address she would have been lost; she would have had no part to play.

'Eat that stew, Kathleen,' she would call, backing it up with a glare. It was mutton stew, with potatoes and onions floating in the thickened parsley sauce. Big helpings were on the plates, and the extra vegetables were piled in white enamelled dishes, like soap dishes. The champagne on Nelly's table seemed absurd. Each time she poured, she looked away, so as not to be seen, and surveyed the road in the rain. Most of the other guests drank soft drinks or milk, but one quiet couple had a bottle of wine. The man who had invited her to the public house ate alone and never once looked in her direction. In fact, when he entered the room he made a show of saluting one or two other people and deliberately ignored her. He drank tumbler after tumbler of milk with his stew. The waitresses, in some show of bravura, had put flowers in their hair, bits of fuchsia, and it was clear by the way they giggled that they thought this to be very scandalous. All the guests resented the interlopers who made such a fuss and such demands – asking for more napkins and for orangeade, some begging to be let down from the table, others slapping their food into plump pancakes, others simply whingeing. A German au pair, who sat among the children, occasionally poured from a water jug but otherwise did not pay much attention to their needs. The waitresses dashed about with second helpings and then brought big slabs of rhubarb pie, each decorated with a whorl of cream so whipped that it seemed like an imitation chef's hat. The owner came into the room and went from table to table – except, of course, to the rowdy table – apologizing to his guests for the invasion, assuring them that it would not happen again. 'End of story ... end of story,' he kept saying, giving the intruders a stern look. The irate mother, sensing rebuff, ordered a pot of tea and a pot of coffee while telling some of her children to go out and play in the grounds. Meanwhile the whipped cream was leaking into the rectangles of rhubarb pie.

All the guests were given a complimentary glass of port wine, and by the time Nelly had finished hers she was the only one left. The room was almost in darkness and it was dark outside. She kept waiting for the candle stump to sputter out, as if that were to be the signal to go upstairs. Already she was thinking that she had only five more dinners to endure and that she would be going home Saturday. Home now seemed like a nest, with its lamps and its warmth. The simpleton gave her a start as he appeared over her, a big clumsy figure in a sheepskin jacket.

'Will you be here tomorrow?' he asked. He had a muffled voice, and there was a stoppage in his speech. It was as if he had too much saliva.

'I'm afraid I will,' she said, and hoped she didn't sound too peeved.

'I'm glad you'll be here. You're a nice lady,' he said as he shuffled out, and, rising, she picked her way between the tables, certain that she was about to break down.

In the morning things seemed quite different – sparkling. The sea was bright, like a mirror with the sun dancing on it, and there was nothing to stop her going down there and spending the whole day walking and breathing – getting rid of the cobwebs, as she put it. She would pack a basket and bring down her things. She would write cards to her sons and her friends; she would read, reread, and, after the few days, she would be something of her former self – cheerful, buoyant, outgoing.

The sand was a pale, biscuit colour that stretched way ahead of her – to the horizon, it seemed. The people dotted here and there were like figures in a primitive painting. Those in red stood out, both the toddlers and the grownups; red was the one splash of colour in this pale-gold, luminous universe. The sea was a baby blue and barely lapped. It seemed so gentle, not like the sea that roared and lashed but like an infinite and glassy terrain that one might scud over. There were dogs, too – the local dogs resenting the dogs that had come with the newcomers, snarling until they got to know them. Some people had erected little tents, obviously intending to settle for the day. Some walked far out to sea, and a few stalwarts were bathing or paddling. Although sunny, it was not yet a hot day. She would walk forever; she would gulp the air with her mouth and her whole being; she would resuscitate herself. Here and there, as she looked down at the sand, she would see empty cans, or seaweed, or little bits of sea holly in clumps – shivering but tenacious.

'I am walking all my bad temper away . . . I am walking

my bad temper away,' she said, and thought, How perfect the isolation, the sense of being alone. She loved it – the near-empty seashore, the stretch of sand, the clouds racing so purposefully, and now the sea itself, which had changed colour as if an intemperate painter had just added blue and green and potent violet. The colours were in pockets, they were in patches, and even as she looked there were transmutations – actual rainbows in the water, shifting, then dissolving. She would walk forever. There wasn't a boat or a steamer in sight. As she looked back at the town, its cluster of white cottages seemed like little rafts on a sea, on the sea of life, receding. People she met smiled or nodded, to compliment her on her stride, and the good thing was that she always saw them as they came toward her, so that she was not taken by surprise. Yet it was a jolt when a woman ran up to her and took her hand. She recognized Nelly from the short time when she had been a television announcer.

'You disappeared so suddenly,' the woman said, and Nelly nodded. She had given up her glamorous job for a man, even though she knew she was throwing in her lot with a black heart.

'We might see you in the pub tonight. There's a singsong,' the woman said, and, though smiling, Nelly quivered inwardly. She did not want to meet people, especially those who had known of her in the past; she had put an iron grille over all that, and yet this very encounter was disturbing, as if the weed and bindweed of the past were pushing their way up through the gates of her mind. As she walked on, she found herself remembering her marriage day – two witnesses and a half bottle of champagne. She remembered living in a big, draughty house in the country, and her morning sickness, which at first she did not understand. But it was as if she were recalling a story that had happened to someone else. In a way, she remembered her divorce far better, because she had had to fight. Once, with a solicitor, she had gone to a suburb of London where she hoped a former housekeeper would testify to her having loved her children; a more recent incumbent had sworn affidavits against her and said she was a wicked woman. In that little sitting room in Tooting, waiting for what was going to be crucial, she sat with the solicitor while the mother put her noisy children to bed. There was a terrible smell, something being cooked.

'Is it a horse they're boiling?' the solicitor said, and she laughed, because she knew he had put himself out of his way to come with her, and that he loved her a little, and that, of course, he would never say so. When the housekeeper came in and kissed her, the kiss itself a guarantee of friendship and loyalty, the solicitor beamed and said, 'We're there . . . we're home and dry.' She got her children in the end. Then there were the years of birthdays and train sets and Christmases and measles and blazers that they grew out of, and then their going away to boarding school and the raw pain of that first rupture, that first farewell. Not for ages had she allowed herself such a glut of memory, such detail.

Yet she was not crushed by these things, and quite gaily she asked aloud what happened to that blue dress with the tulip line, and where was the Georgian claret jug that she had bought for a song. Where, oh where?

Up on the road, there were several cars and a loudspeaker announcing something. Although it was loud, it was senseless. She was a long way from the hotel but she had her bearings. She knew she could either turn right to head for the one shop and the telephone kiosk or turn left for her hotel and the new chapel beyond it, which had modern stained-glass windows. She felt hot and her throat was parched – she longed for something. She believed that she longed for lemonade. She could taste it again as she had tasted it in childhood, so sweet and yet so tart. The sun shone with a flourish, and the flowers in the cottage gardens – the dahlias, or the devil's pokers, or whatever – seemed to be glistening with life. She stopped by a garden where a yearling calf was letting out a loud lament. He had two wounds where his horns had recently been removed. They were full of flies. He tried with his head to toss them away, but they had sunk into the wounds, which were covered with some sort of purple ointment. The animal bawled and tossed and even leapt about, and so moved was she to pity that she began to shout, 'Are you there? Are you there?'

Eventually a young man came out, holding a mug of tea. He seemed surprised to have been called.

'He's itchy,' she said, pointing to the yearling.

'He's a devil,' the young man said.

'He's in agony,' she said, and asked if he could do something.

'What can I do?' he said, annoyed that she had summoned him like this.

'I'll help you,' she said, gently, to coax him.

'I have just the thing,' he said, and he ran to the house and came back with a giant canister of wasp repellent.

'Oh, not that,' she said, grabbing it from him and explaining that the flies would wallow in the wounds and dement the poor animal even more. She made him fetch a strip of cardboard, then hold the beast, which bucked and reared while she edged the flies out pushing them onto the clay and watching them stagger from their somersaults. The man was so impressed by her expertise that he asked if she was a vet.

'Hold him, hold him,' she said, as there was the second wound that she had to tackle. That done, they drove the animal through a side gate, over some cobbles, and into a dark manger. As the man closed the door, the animal yelled to be let out, its cry saying that daylight, even delirious daylight with flies and pain, was preferable to this dark dungeon.

'I told you he was a devil. He never lets up,' the man said, as he motioned her into the house. There was nobody in there, he assured her, his mother being dead. The few flowers in the flowerbed, and the gooseberry bushes, had, as she imagined, been sown by his mother. There was also a ridge of flowering potatoes. He went to England for a time, worked in a car factory there, but he always came back in the summer, because he needed the fresh air. He bought a calf or two and sold them when he left.

'Would you marry me?' he said suddenly. She knew that he did not really mean such a thing, that he meant 'Stay for a bit and talk to me.'

'I am married,' she lied.

'You've no wedding ring,' he said, and she looked down at her hand and smiled, and said she must have forgotten to put it on. Then she excused herself, saying that she had to be back at the hotel, because of a phone call.

Caimin met her at the door. She had had a visitor, a woman. The woman had waited and waited. He handed her a note. It said 'Hi. Long time no see. I'll call back around four. Gertie.' Who was Gertie? Gertrude. She could only think of *Hamlet*. Suddenly she was shaking. She could not see anyone. She did not want to meet this Gertie, this stranger.

'Tell her I've gone ... gone,' she said as she flew up the stairs to her room. Even the disgruntled neighbour, who was on his way out, seemed to sense her disquiet. He smiled, and waved a golf club, proudly. She hated the hotel even more now – the awful washbasin, the stained furniture. She hated it not so much for its own pitiable sake as for what it reminded her of – the rooms and landings of childhood, basins and slop buckets that oozed sadness. It seemed as if the furniture of those times, and her failed marriage, and the flies in the raw wounds, and the several mistakes of her life had got jumbled together and were now hounding her, moving in on her in this place. Various suggestions offered themselves, such as to go back to London to her own house and never leave it again, or to go to the house where she was born and exorcise her fury, though she had been back there a few times and was almost indifferent to the sight of it. She saw briars, she saw gates in need of paint, she saw the outside gable wall over which her mother had so lovingly planted a creeper, and she saw the hall door with the padlocks that her brother had put there to keep her and others out. Bastard, she thought, and wished she could scrawl it somewhere for him to see. Her maggot brother.

'This won't do,' she said, sitting on the bed, reliving old hatreds, fresh and vigorous as when first incurred. Coming back had set off this further welter of rage, like a time bomb.

'What is it?' she asked aloud, wondering what particle in the brain is triggered by some smell, or the wind, or a yearling in pain, or a voice sodden with loneliness that says, without meaning it, 'Would you marry me?'

She might have known it: there was a knock on the door, Caimin calling her, saying she had a visitor, saying it with excitement, as if she should be pleased. He had completely misunderstood her instructions, her clamour to be left alone. Out she went, fuming, about to tell him to send the stranger away, but the stranger was standing there beside him – a largish woman in a raincoat, with grey hair drawn back severely in a bun. 'Hay fever,' Nelly heard herself saying, to account for the tears, and for the crumpled handkerchief that she was holding. Caimin left them together on the landing and shuffled off like a dog that knows it has done something wrong.

'You don't remember me,' the woman was saying. She was breathless, as if she had run, so eager was she to be there. Bringing her face closer, she allowed Nelly to scan it, pleased to present this challenge. Nelly realized it must be someone from her nearby home. She tried to recall all her school friends, tried to picture them at their desks, or in the choir on Sundays, or in the school photo that they had all received when they left. This face was not among them.

'No,' she said finally, feeling a little baffled.

'I'm Gertie . . . Mrs Conway's niece. She owned the hotel in your town,' the woman said with a nervous smile. Her excitement was fading and she realized that she was not welcome. She began apologizing for barging in, explaining that a woman in the shop said she had seen Nelly Nugent walking on the seashore.

'Mrs Conway's niece,' Nelly said, trying not to bristle. Of course. Gertie's aunt had also owned a house here. They used to come for weekends, had houseparties.

'Gertie,' she whispered, remembering the vivid young girl who had come often to stay at her aunt's hotel. She had served behind the counter like a grownup, and had the opportunity to meet all the men, to flirt with them. Being Gertie, she had snatched the prize of them all.

Yes, she remembered Gertie. She remembered precisely when she had first seen Gertie – unexpectedly, as it happened. She was about to leave her home village, to go to the town to learn shorthand, and an older girl – Eileen, who lived up the country – had promised her a dress that she had become too fat to wear. It was black grosgrain and it had long sleeves – that was all she knew. She walked to Eileen's on a summer's day, after lunch, and twice had to ask the way, as there was more than one family of the same name. She remembered that she had to cross a stream to get to the house, and, yielding to a bit of fancy because of the sunshine and the thought of the dress, she took off her shoes and dipped her feet in the water, which she felt to be like liquid silver washing over her insteps and toes. The dress fit her perfectly. In fact, it fit her so well and gave her such allure that Eileen put her arms around her and, almost in tears, said, 'Hold on to your looks, Nell. Whatever you do, hold on to your looks.' That was thirty-odd years ago. Walking down the country road, all alone, she was so sure of herself and her beauty then; she even believed that the trees and the gates and the walls and the brambles partook of it. Along with the dress, Eileen had given her an old handbag, in which there was a little mirror with a tortoiseshell frame, and from time to time, she ran the looking-glass down the length of the dress to see the flare and the grosgrain reflected.

As she neared the town, she decided to do it. It would have been inconceivable on the way up to the country, but now she was a different person – sophisticated, assured – and anyhow she was going away. She decided to seek him out at his lodgings. It was a house not far from the chapel – one of the five or six terraced houses with a tiled hallway and a stained-glass fanlight over the door that shone ruby or blue or green floating patterns on the floor, depending on the position of the sun. The landlady, a thin and inquisitive woman, answered the timid knock, and upon hearing the request said, 'He's having his tea.' Nelly stood her ground; she had come to see him and she was not going away without seeing him. He was the new teacher in the technical college and had many skills. He was swarthy and handsome and he had made an impression on most of the young girls and the women. Many had boasted of having had conversations with him, and promises to learn tennis from him, or woodwork, or the piano accordion. 'I won't keep him long,' she said to the landlady, who was running her tongue all around her teeth, before deciding to consider the request.

He sauntered toward her – his red sweater seeming so dashing – with a puzzled smile on his face. The moment he stood in front of her with that look of pleasant inquiry, she registered two things: that his eyes were a dark green that gave the semblance of brown, and that she was not going to be able to say why she had called on him, had him routed from his tea table. She saw, too, that his eyes took in every feature of her, that he knew why she had come, knew that she was smitten, knew that she was embarrassed, and felt a certain animal pleasure, a triumph, in those things, and was not in the least bit discomfited. He stood there smiling, studying her face, not in any hurry to break the silence.

'I wondered about your night classes,' she said, even though he, like everybody else, had probably heard the news that she was going to the city to train as a secretary. 'I mean, my mother wondered,' she then said, becoming even clumsier by adding that her mother felt that women should be able to take the woodwork class just the same as men.

'Agreed,' he said with that pleased, tantalizing smile. Indeed, one little cautionary part of her recognized him as being rather smug, but it was not enough to dampen the flush of attraction and excitement that she felt toward him. She had felt it for weeks, ever since he came – sighting him on his way to or from Mass, or on his bicycle, or in his tweed jacket with the leather patches on the elbows, or on the hurley pitch in his togs, where he stumbled and fell but always got up again to tackle an opponent. It was obviously time for her to leave, because she had said her piece. Yet she lingered. He put a finger to his teeth where a piece of rasin had stuck. Raisins, he declared, were the bane of his life, as he picked at assiduously. Then, from the kitchen, she heard his name called: 'Vincent ... Vince.' It was not the landlady's voice, it was another voice – coyer and younger. Then, in the doorway, Gertie appeared – a girl a bit older than herself – running her hands up and down the jamb, caressing it and smiling at them. She wore trousers that clung to her. They were of a black hairy stuff, like angora. She was like a cat. Like a cat, she stroked the door, ran her fingers along it as if she were running them over his body. He basked for a moment in the excitement of it, poised as he was between two doting creatures – one assured, the other lamentably awkward.

'Your tea is getting cold,' Gertie said.

'How cold?' he asked, amused.

'So-so cold,' she said saucily.

'He always talked about you,' Gertie was saying to her now, as if she guessed every particle of thought that had passed in a swoop through Nelly's mind. 'When we had a card party or a Christmas party, he always boasted that he knew you. You were a feather in his cap, especially after you appeared on television.'

'How is he? ... How are you?' Nelly asked. She remembered hearing about their engagement, their lavish wedding preparations, and especially their coming to this very spot for a prolonged honeymoon. In fact, without her realizing it, in some recess of her mind, this place was always their preserve.

'Oh, he died ... Didn't you know? He died suddenly ...' Gertie said very quietly, her voice trailing off, suggesting that there were many other things she would have liked to say, such as what his death had meant to her, and how happy or unhappy their marriage had been.

'He liked the ladies,' she said then. There was something

so incredibly gentle about it that all of a sudden Nelly embraced her and invited her to stay and have tea, or a drink, or whatever.

'I can't,' Gertie said, and explained that a woman friend had driven over with her for the day, and that the woman was outside, waiting in the car. 'Another time,' she said. But they both knew that there would probably not be another time.

'And you kept the figure,' Gertie said, then drew her coat open to show her own girth, to pay Nelly a belated compliment. Then she was gone, hurrying down the stairs, the belt and buckle of her open raincoat trailing behind her.

Nelly stood stunned, tears in her eyes. She felt as if doors or windows were swinging open all around her and that she was letting go of some awful affliction. Something had happened. She did not know what it was. But soon she would know. Soon she would feel as she had felt long ago – like a river that winds its way back into its first beloved enclave before finally putting out to sea.

A DEMON

IT WAS A BIG DAY. Yes, this was the day they were going to visit her brother in the monastery and then go on to a convent, sixty miles from there, where her sister was repining and was going to have to be brought home. No one knew exactly what was wrong with her sister. She had had pleurisy, which had lingered, and now the nuns feared that she had tuberculosis. She languished, and would not get out of bed at all. Yet the day itself loomed with a flush of happiness: the monastery and the monks, and their legendary brown bread with tea in the big refectory, and maybe a sight of the silkworms – because, yes, they had silkworms, not that she understood the workings of these creatures – and no doubt a little shop with the most delicate mother-of-pearl rosary beads, as well as the dark, horn ones, and holy pictures of saints and martyrs in tints that made their expressions both fetching and tragic. They would of course pray in the draughty chapel, with the monks in brown all around them, heads bowed, meditating, never stirring to look at the strangers. She might even meet the abbot and kiss his ring; suddenly, the thought of kissing the ring of an abbot or a bishop made her shudder with terror that she would take a bite out of it by mistake.

They had hired a car, and this time it was not the local pup, who showed up whenever it suited him, but an older man who rarely drove a hackney. Although he would charge them more, he was, in a sense, doing them a favour, as her father said. The price was agreed. Her father had told her mother the amount and he had it ready in one pocket, with some change in the other pocket in case they stopped to have coffee or lemonade or had to give an offering for a Mass. The most wonderful thing about the day was that they would not be on their own. They were not just mother, father and daughter Meg, with father likely to throw a tantrum at any minute and tell the driver to stop the car at a public house and go in, not for a coffee but for a few whiskeys, and commence on a batter that would last for weeks and would be perfidious. No, they were to have a visitor, a very important woman, the most suave and dashing woman in the whole town – the doctor's wife. She had a dark fur coat with lighter stripes in it, and matching gloves. She had a very thin, sallow face and gold bracelets that had slipped up above her elbow and could not be wedged down, so that she wore them even in bed under her nightie. She was called Kitty, and indeed had not always been friendly with them; in fact, she had snubbed them for years, but, as Meg's mother said, age mellows people. Her mother was thrilled. For all those years she had tried to effect a friendship, sending gifts of cakes and eggs, and once she compromised herself seriously. It was with Kitty's eldest daughter, who was also called Kitty, and who took to making jaunts to their house on her bicycle, befriending them for an entire summer.

Meg's mother had three pieces of silk, each one being the length of a summer dress; she had had them for years. She would hold them up against the children, not actually promising them anything, because she felt that these pieces of silk were too special. And then it so happened that young Kitty came along, made a habit of calling on them, was given powdered lemonade and cake while sitting on a card chair in the front of the house – sitting in a niche between two walls of jutting stone, where the sun, if it ever shone, was likely to light on her. Kitty had such a way of attracting attention that everyone was mesmerized by her. One day when she was there, rattling on about some happy thing she had done, Meg's mother rose from her stool all of a sudden, dashed through the vestibule, went up the stairs, obviously intent on something important. She was back in a short time, holding one of those pieces of material in her two hands the way she might hold a rosary. Kitty gasped with delight, said, 'What a gorgeous colour. Golden. Or is it apricot?'

'Have it!' Meg's mother said, and added, 'It will make you think of us.'

Kitty took and smelled it, and made such a show of gratitude that the mother was ecstatic. First Kitty held it up to herself, letting the bottom half trail on the gravel, which unnerved Meg's mother; then she gathered it all up and wrapped it around her, sari-like, and then she wore it as a shawl, covering her brown hair and letting it fall over her shoulders in bright golden cascades. It was yellow stuff with gooseberries and cowslips of paler yellow spattered throughout. Kitty's gratitude was so great that it was like a moment not out of normal life but out of a play. She kissed the material, she embraced the mother, she complimented her on having the best taste of any woman in the parish, including her own mother, she discussed possible styles and wondered if there were enough for a coatee; then again she said she did not think she could take it, and contradicted herself by holding on to it with both hands, as if someone were snatching it from her.

For a moment, the mother forgot that she had given something very precious away. Most likely she thought that the friendship was now indestructible, and that in the future she might look out of the window at any moment and say, 'Kitty's mother is coming!' But, far more than that, Meg's mother hoped that she would be asked to their house. She would walk up the street on Sunday evening in her best costume and the shoes that crippled her, and be the one to knock on their knocker, which the maid polished religiously Mondays, Wednesdays and Fridays. She had never been inside that house; no local person had, because Kitty's mother found the local people uncouth, she having come from the city. It was said they had beautiful furniture, a hall stand, Spanish chests where they kept their linen, and a clock that could be heard chiming on the days when the front door was open while the maid was polishing the knocker. They had had parties, but these parties were for people from the city and even abroad.

Kitty took the dress material home in a rush basket, and was not to be seen for the rest of the week. It was, of course, not long before the mother repented her impulse, because now that Kitty had got something out of her she did not call again. A few weeks later, she even came close to snubbing the family, simply by darting back into her own house as they passed by for the evening Rosary. It would have been the perfect opportunity for an informal visit, for Kitty to say, 'Take us as we are,' to call her mother from the kitchen or the bedroom or wherever she was and usher them into the front room to sit them on the high velvet sofa that swayed, it was said, like a hammock and was the colour of bulrushes. Even Meg imagined them going in. She imagined that Kitty only closed the door for a second, having got such a shock, but that, after an interval, the door would open again and they would step into the hall, and either Kitty or her mother would say, 'My, my, to think you'd never been here before! I thought you had!' And then they would go into that carpeted precinct, and, after another decent interval, the cupboard with the green lattice front would be opened, and bottles and tinted glasses would be taken out, and Kitty's mother would say, 'What's your poison? Will you have the hard stuff or cordials?' It was not to be. Their hall door, painted a dark oxblood red, was pushed to as her mother and she passed by. It was done very pointedly, and Meg's mother quickened her pace, and said that the last thing she ever wanted was for them to think that she begged or wished for their hospitality.

'They even count the number of potatoes before they put them in the pot!' the mother said, a way of denouncing them. She was hurt. She was so hurt that she never prayed during the Rosary, and on the way home she kept saying cutting things about people in general – how people had no heart, how people would take from you and then close the door on you – but the little girl knew whom she meant. The friendship was made up much later, at a funeral. A mutual friend had died young, and death, as the mother said sorrowfully, binds all. They sat together at the wake and whispered.

The car was due at eleven, but it was now one o'clock and it had not come. The harmony of the morning was going somewhat askew, as Meg could hear from the arguing within. Her father was saying God blast it, that he couldn't rely on anyone, and where in the name of blazes was the bloke? And her mother was saying that instead of getting on his high horse it would be far more sensible to go over to the town and find the man.

'Tramp over there in my good clothes?' the father said.

'Change your clothes!' she said.

And in protest he took off his tie, and then they resumed looking through the window. Soon the little girl was called in to have a slice of bread, which she didn't want, and she saw tears in her mother's eyes, and her mother said that whenever she looked forward to anything it was always botched, and that she had lived for this day and that the doctor's wife would be on edge, too, probably in the hallway with her coat on, pacing and wondering. Meg's father threatened not to go at all, to which her mother said that if the driver didn't come soon there would be no point in any of them going. Because first they had to go north to one county, spend some time there, and then retrace their steps and go west to another county. She estimated the mileage while the father made himself a mug of tea that was dark as treacle. Their spirits lifted once when the dog barked, but it was a false alarm. Finally it was decided that they would go to the gate and wait there, to save a few minutes, or, as the child thought, to forestall her father from going up to bed in a sulk. At the gate they met a farmer, whom they asked to call on the hackney driver, to tell him to 'buck up'.

'Who would that be?' the farmer asked in a slow voice. He was told three times, but didn't seem to grasp it.

'Ape,' her mother said, as the man geed up his horse. He had given Meg a penny, very new and shiny, with the lines of the harp so clear and sharp they looked like pieces of slanted thread. She squeezed it in her palm, hoping that it could get green from the copper – to be one with it.

'Jaysus, I couldn't help it. I was under her for an hour,' the driver said as the black, bulky car came to a standstill along the kerb. Meg's father rushed forward to open the door and gives James, the driver, a pasting. The doctor's wife, Kitty, sat in the back, looking a little quiet and irked, and then the mother got in beside her and apologized. Meg sat at Kitty's other side, and the two men in front, where the prevailing mood was soon alleviated when they lit up cigarettes. The car got hot, the windows foggy in the cold, and she felt as if she were in some house or buggy going far, far away from their own place, and that in this big travelling room with the mahogany dashboard and tartan rugs they all cleaved together, chatting and cracking jokes. Her father was making jokes about the car now, and about James being 'under her' for half the morning. Whenever there were people with them, they were much livelier and happier, so if they could be with James and the doctor's wife forever that would be the solution. The doctor's wife had thawed a bit also, and was smiling, and when the mother leaned over and touched Meg's wrist and said, 'We were very put out', the doctor's wife gave the child a little smile, and it was as if one of the saints, out of the rich assortment of holy pictures in her prayer book, had smiled at her or given her recognition.

'We even made a novena,' her mother said and laughed; it was really to get the doctor's wife to laugh that she did it. Meg was annoyed that her mother should reveal a secret of hers, especially a secret about promises made to God. Yes, she had offered to make a sacrifice if the car came, which she now regretted. She would not eat apple tart, she would also decline lemonade if it was offered her, and that night, when they got home, she would get out of bed at least ten times to say several Our Fathers, Hail Marys and Glorias.

They passed a few strange towns, where people looked at them with a certain curiosity. Meg's father knew some of the people in these towns, because he had drunk in them, and although this was a scourge to her mother and a source of tribulation, she now made jokes about her husband's popularity and said that he ought to stand for Parliament, he knew so many people.

'That's the thruth,' the driver said, and Meg's father laughed. Good humour reigned. They would drive forever – forget her brother, forget her sister, go to no monastery, no convent, but rather to some undestined place. She loved her sister, yes. But there was a 'but'; it was a terrible 'but'. She had seen her sister and a man over by the public house. They stood very close together, side by side, but her sister's gabardine was up at the back, and the man's hand groping under it, and they were breathing in a funny way, the two of them. That was a bad thing, a very bad thing. Something told her so, even though she did not know exactly what was going on, and her sister was sick now – dying, maybe. No wonder.

The doctor's wife was engaging them with talk about a film she had seen with her husband and another couple. They had driven to Limerick and had first had supper in a very nice restaurant, and the trouble was that none of them felt inclined to leave the table, forego the wine and cigarettes and so forth, to see slush – as the doctor referred to it. She always called her husband 'the doctor', even to his face. He was quite abrupt, but the locals liked him, said he was good at diagnosing, and very thorough. It was said that he kissed nurses, but no one accused him of it, knowing that they would want him in their hour of need. The film they went to had a mixed reception among them – the women liking it, the men not.

'Too romantic,' Kitty said and made a face. She sucked her cheeks in, maybe to resemble the heroine of the film. The child thought that beneath the sleeves of Kitty's fur coat and the nice fuzzy pink dress she was wearing for the occasion were the bracelets, grazing her skin.

They arrived late at the monastery. The monk had to explain that lunch was officially over but he had kept soup and bread. It was a green soup made of nettles, and she was afraid that it would sting her. Her mother said wasn't it marvellous to use something as useless as nettles, then asked the monk in a quiet voice if perhaps she could have the recipe. The bread was nutty, and while they were eating, two monks sat with them and talked agriculture with Meg's father. The doctor's wife wasn't eating at all, and at one point whispered to the mother, 'I could do with a gin,' and the mother said that on their way over to the convent they would stop at Portumna.

The son was called out from his class, and as they stood on the refectory steps with the wind whipping around them, making the gravel shiver, he told his parents that he had decided upon a profession – he wanted to be a doctor. Their eyes filled up with tears, although later, in the car, Meg's mother said, 'How in the name of God are we going to afford it? University fees, digs in Dublin, train fare, then books for his study, and so on and on, not to mention his outfits!' Meg's father said to leave it to him, and her mother raised her eyes.

The visit had been very short because of having to go to the next place before the nuns went to bed; the nuns went to bed at nine. It was dark now, and what Meg saw along the road were fields that stretched to the sky, with here and there a star to light the immensity of the gloom. It seemed to her that those few stars shone deliberately to give voyagers, such as them, a ray of hope. She thought of the Magi.

They stopped at a hotel in Portumna, and Meg's mother went to great trouble to get the drink for the doctor's wife. It had, of course, to be in secret. She left Kitty in the hall and found a young porter with a brass-buttoned uniform, and asked him to 'fetch it up'. She stationed herself on the landing, the money in her hand, but, as it turned out, not enough money, because there had to be a tonic with the gin. The little girl had to cough up the extra sixpence, but she was proud to do it and only hoped that the doctor's wife would learn of it, so that she would get a smile of gratitude. Kitty drank it up quickly and with evident pleasure and said that it was such a boost. It was clear that she wanted another, so Meg's mother said, 'Don't budge!'

and, in secret, she borrowed all the money the little girl had, then ran off, returning with a second drink under her scarf. Her happiness was immense, as well as her pride in being able to please this woman whom for years she had sought to know. She had been hurt, of course, but all was forgiven, and they planned on a day out to Limerick together, with no men to addle them. They were friends for life now – their lithe conspiracy had bound them.

Afterward, they joined the men in the lounge downstairs, where they had tea and biscuits. Meg's mother marvelled at a mirror, a big overmantel in a gold frame with gold roses and garlands of ivy encircling it. A crack in the surface of the mirror had been camouflaged with flowers that zigzagged, like a river. The mother said that to her dying day she would never forget the ingenuity of that. The little girl broke her pledge and ate biscuits and knew even as she was doing it that bad luck would befall her before the day was out. They were coconut biscuits, and as much as she loved them and gorged on the white shreds she also hated them, because she had defected from her resolve. Her father dipped his biscuit in the tea and sucked it. The driver ate the sandwiches. They left in such a hurry that she forgot her coat – a navy nap coat with seamed leather buttons. Her mother was so furious with her in the car that she thumped her and said, 'What demon got into you, to come away without your best coat?' Meg cried, and said 'Sorry' a number of times, and her father said that they would get the coat. He knew the owner of the hotel; they'd telephone the next day, and it could be put on the bus.

'All that bother!' her mother said, and thumped again, and she cried so loud that the doctor's wife leaned across and lent her a hankie; it was a silk hankie with lace edging, and it had 'Souvenir of Paris' embroidered on it. Her mother finally forgave her as they neared the convent.

They had gone astray, which caused them to lose an hour; the driver had taken the wrong road and was heading towards home when he said, 'Jaysus!' and reversed to a crossroads where there was a batch of signs. He got out to read them and came back and told of his error.

'It could happen to a bishop,' Meg's father said, but her mother was not pleased. The convent shut at nine, and there was no way they could drive again the next day to fetch their daughter. Not much sympathy was evinced for the daughter's illness, at least not yet. She was a wilful girl, and had often filched her mother's dance dresses and fal-lals, and when she came home on holiday she slept late, then got up, had a big breakfast and went off gallivanting. She was not a homebody.

The gatekeeper grumbled, said he had been looking out for them all night and that most of the nuns had gone up to bed, except for two. They were very cheerful nuns, who gripped the hands of their visitors and said they must be perished, and ushered them into a parlour where there was tea laid out on a trolley – tea and sponge cake. The tea was in a flask and the sponge cake was like a jewel – dusted over with fine sugar, the jam oozing out at the sides and trickling down over the yellow tier. They sat on big carved chairs and waited while one of the nuns went to fetch Meg's sister, Nancy. She came in with the nuns, a blanket wrapped all around her, looking very listless. She kissed her parents, kissed the doctor's wife, and then sat and coughed. Her father asked her if she was all right, and one of the nuns said that she would be when she got home and had good dinners of bacon and cabbage, and plenty of fresh air, and she repeated the proverb that there was no place like home. She said that Nancy was the brightest girl in all of Ireland and could sweep the country in examinations, and that she must get well and strong in order to make her mark. The driver had not come in, because although they had been chummy with him in the hotel they thought it was bad form to have him in a convent parlour, seeing nuns at that hour of the night. The cake was so delicious that Meg had two pieces, and her mother touched her tummy and said that if she ate any more she would be like a little barrel. The funny thing was that when the blanket slipped off once and she caught a look at her sister, her tummy was like a little barrel. She thought it odd for a sick girl to have such a corporation.

The doctor's wife saw it, too, and said, 'Have you put on weight, Nancy?' Nancy said it was fluids. She had fluids on her lungs and they had travelled down. Meg felt very queer all of a sudden, as if she were being turned inside out on a skewer, the way she always felt when she got a fright. She knew then that some terrible thing was going to befall them, and she even made the wish that they would crash on the way home – go into a wall, all of them, die together before this worse calamity happened.

The driver had to go very slowly because of fog, and they had all run out of conversation, so it was a silent, anxious journey as the car crawled along, and from time to time the driver had to stop to look at the signs. When they finally reached their own gate, the mother apologized to the doctor's wife for not asking her in, grieving at the lateness of the hour. Inside, the house was cold, and the dog rushed in after them, yelping for food. The mother fetched the torch and told the father to go and shut the hens. He asked Meg to go with him, because he was afraid to go to the yard at night alone, but he pretended it was just for company's sake. In their coop, the hens clucked and made as if to leave their perches, thinking because of the glimmer of light that it was morning, and one got out in spite of them. There was a smell of soft, warm dung, and this, along with the low croak of the hens, made her envious of their existence, which she saw as trouble-free. He said they weren't to tell Mother that a hen had got out, as she would be raging.

Inside, the invalid had gone to bed; her mother said, 'She was all in,' and expressed pity for her, for the first time. The father had tea and bread, and, as there was school next day, Meg put a bit of polish on her shoes – but only at the saluting part of her shoes. She was sleeping in the same room as her sister; she dreaded it and hoped that Nancy was in bed by now and fast asleep. She did not want to see her undressed. Her mother told her to carry up a cup of cocoa for her poor sister and say her prayers, and that she had been a good girl, apart from the incident with the coat. Her father put what was left of his change on the dresser and said that James, the driver, could break the bank of Monte Carlo with the amount of sandwiches he consumed.

In the bedroom, Nancy was crying. She was in dreadful pain. She said it was appendicitis, she knew it was. Other girls at school had had it, and unless the appendix was taken out she would die of peritonitis. Between each sentence she gripped the quilt – first with her hands and then, as the pain got worse, with her teeth. Then she paused and waited for another spasm to overtake her. Meg knew different; she knew it was not appendicitis – she knew without knowing, like the day she knew without knowing what it was when she saw her sister with her gabardine coat up at the back. However, she was not going to say it. She had just taken a vow of silence, and she did not answer her sister's pleas to help her, to go downstairs and tell them that she needed a doctor, as she had an appendix that was on the point of bursting. She would not do it, she could not do it. The doctor would come and all would be revealed.

'Please, please, little mite!' her elder sister begged, the tears rolling down her face and her mouth opening and shutting to alleviate the spasms.

'Let's say a prayer,' Meg said, relenting.

In a few hours' time, their lives would be destroyed, she thought. There was no knowing what would happen. It was awful. Possibly one if not two people would get killed; this new arrival would be done away with first. She saw it as a monster with two heads. She heard it in her mind's ear – bawling, then quelled. The longer she delayed going to the landing to call, the longer she could postpone the catastrophe. But at that moment her sister let out a cry so piercing no one could avoid hearing it, and as Meg rushed out onto the landing she met her mother, and she knew with a terrible clarity that her mother knew, because she said, 'The demon, the demon, what has she done?' As her mother rushed into the room, her angry voice was swamped by a series of roars that forestalled any further questioning . . . and it was clear now that the doctor would have to be summoned.

'I'll put water on to boil,' Meg said, and then she began to hum in a loud, screechy voice. In no time at all their house would be a battlefield.

DRAMAS

When the new shopkeeper arrived in the village he aroused great curiosity along with some scorn. He was deemed refined because his fingernails looked as if they had been varnished a tinted ivory. He had a horse, or as my father was quick to point out, a glorified pony, which he had brought from the Midlands, where he had previously worked. The pony was called Daisy, a name unheard of in our circles for an animal. The shopkeeper wore a long black coat, a black hat, talked in a low voice, made his own jams and marmalades, and could even darn and sew. All that we came to know of, in due course, but at first we knew him only as Barry. In time the shop would have his name, printed in beautiful silver sloping script, above the door. He had bought the long-disused bakery, had all the ovens thrown out, and turned it into a palace which not only had gadgets but gadgets that worked, a lethal slicer for the ham, a new kind of weighing scale that did not require iron weights hefted on to one side but that simply registered the weight of a bag of meal and told it by a needle that spun round, wobbling dementedly before coming to a standstill. Even farmers praised its miraculous skills. He also had a meat safe with a grey gauze door, a safe in which creams and cheeses could be kept fresh for an age, free of the scourge of flies or gnats.

Straight away he started to do great business as the people reneged on the shops where they had dealt for years and where many of them owed money. They flocked, to look at him, to hear his well-mannered voice and to admire dainties and things that he had in stock. He had ten different flavoured jellies and more than one brand of coffee. The women especially liked him. He leaned over the counter, discussing things with them, their headaches, their knitting, patterns for suits or dresses that they might make, and along with that he kept an open tin of biscuits so that they could have them if they felt peckish. The particular favourite was a tiny round biscuit, like a holy communion wafer with a thin skin of rice paper as a lining. These were such favourites that Barry would have to put his hand down beneath the ruffs of ink paper and ferret up a few from the bottom. The rice paper did not taste like paper at all but like a disc of some magical metamorphosed sugar. Besides that coveted biscuit, there were others, a sandwich of ginger with a soft white filling that was as sturdy as putty, and another in which there was a blend of raspberry and custard, a combination that engendered such ecstasy that one was torn between the pleasure of devouring it or tasting each grain slowly so as to isolate the raspberry from the custard flavour. There were also arrowroot and digestives, but these were the last to be eaten. He called the biscuits 'bikkies' and cigarettes 'ciggies'.

He was not such a favourite with the men, both because he raved to the women and because he voiced the notion of bringing drama to the town. He said that he would find a drama that would embody the talents of the people and that he would direct and produce it himself. Constantly he was casting people, and although none of us knew precisely what he meant, we would agree when he said, 'Rosalind, a born Rosalind,' or, 'Cordelia, if ever I met one.' He did not, however, intend to do Shakespeare, as he feared that, being untrained, the people would not be able to get their tongues around the rhyming verse and would not feel at home in bulky costumes. He would choose something more suitable, something that people could identify with. Every time he went to the city to buy stock, he also brought one or two plays, and if there was a slack moment in the shop he would read a speech or even a whole scene, he himself acting the parts, the men's and the women's. He was very convincing when he acted the women or the girls. One play was about a young girl who saw a dead seagull and in seeing it, her tragedy was predestined. She was crossed in love, had an illegitimate child and drove a young man to suicide. Another time he read scenes about two very unhappy people in Scandinavia who scalded each other, daily, with accusation and counter-accusation, and to buoy himself up, the man did a frenzied dance. Barry did the dance, too, jumping on and off the weighing scales or even onto the counter when he got carried away. He used to ask me to stay on after the shop closed, simply because I was as besotted as he was by these exotic and tormented characters. It was biscuits, sweets, lemonade, anything. Yet something in me trembled, foresaw trouble.

The locals were suspicious, they did not want plays about dead birds and illegitimate children, or unhappy couples tearing at each other, because they had these scenarios aplenty. Barry decided, wisely, to do a play that would be more heartening, a simple play about wholesome people and wholesome themes, such as getting the harvest in safely. I was always privy to each new decision, partly because of my mania for the plays and partly because I had to tell him how his pony was doing. The pony grazed with us and consequently we were given quite a lot of credit. I shall never forget my mother announcing this good news to me flushed with pride, almost suave as she said, 'If ever you have the hungry grass on the way from school, just go into Barry and say you feel like a titbit.' By her telling me this so casually, I saw how dearly she would have loved to have been rich, to entertain, to give lunch parties and supper parties, to show off the linen tablecloths and the good cutlery which she had Vaselined over the years to keep the steel from rusting. In these imaginary galas she brandished the two silver salvers, the biscuit barrel and the dinner plates with their bouquets of violets in the centre and scalloped edging that looked like crochet work. We had been richer, but over the years the money got squandered.

Barry wisely did not talk to her about dramas but about the ornaments in our house, commenting on her good taste. It was the happiest half year in my life, being able to linger in Barry's shop and while he was busy read some of these plays and act them silently inside my head. With the customers all gone, I would sit on the counter, swing my legs, gorge biscuits and discuss both the stories and the characters. Barry in his white shop coat and with a sharpened pencil in his hands would make notes of the things we said. He would discuss the scenery, the lights, intonation of each line, and when an actor should hesitate or then again when an actor should let rip. Barry said it was a question of contrast, of nuance versus verve. I stayed until dark, until the moon came up or the first star. He walked home, but he did not try to kiss one or put his hand on the tickly part at the back of the knee, the way other men did, even the teacher's first cousin, who pretended he wasn't doing it when he was. Barry was as pure as a young priest and like a priest had pale skin with down on it. His only blemish was his thinning hair, and the top of head was like an egg, with big wisps, which I did not like to look at.

Business for him was not quite as flush as in those first

excitable weeks, but as he would say to my mother, things were 'ticking over', and also he was lucky in that his Aunt Milly in the Midlands was going to leave him her farm and her house. Meanwhile, if there were debts she would come to the rescue, so that he would never be, disgraced by having his name printed in a gazette where all the debtors' names were printed so that the whole country knew of it.

As it neared autumn Barry had decided on a play and had started auditions. 'All for Hecuba and Hecuba for me,' he said to the mystified customers. It was a play about travelling players, so that, as he said, the actors and actresses could have lots of verve and camp it up. No one knew quite what he meant by 'camp it up'. He mulled over playing the lead himself, but there were objections from people in the town. So each evening men and women went to the parlour that adjoined the shop, read for him and often emerged disgruntled and threatening to start up a rival company because he did not give them the best part. Then an extraordinary thing happened. Barry had written on the spur of the moment to a famous actor in Dublin for a spot of advice. In the letter he had also said that if the actor was ever passing through the vicinity he might like 'to break bread'. Barry was very proud of the wording of this letter. The actor replied on a postcard. It was a postcard on which four big white cats adhered together, in a mesh. Spurred by this signal Barry made a parcel of country stuffs and sent them to the actor by registered post. He sent butter, fowl, homemade cake and eggs wrapped in thick twists of newspaper and packed in a little papier-mâché box.

Not long after, I met him in the street, in a dither. The most extraordinary thing had happened. The actor and his friend were coming to visit, had announced it without being invited, said they had decided to help Barry in his artistic endeavour and would teach him all the rudiments of theatre that were needed for his forthcoming production.

'A business lunch *à trois*,' was how Barry described it, his voice three octaves higher, his face unable to disguise his fervid excitement. My mother offered to lend linen and cutlery, the Liddy girl was summoned to scrub, and Oona, the sacristan, was cajoled to part with some of the flowers meant for the altar, while I was enlisted to go around the hedges and pick anything, leaves, branches, anything.

'His friend is called Ivan,' Barry said, and added that, though Ivan was not an actor, he was a partner and saw to the practical aspect of things. How he knew this I have no idea, because I doubt that the actor would have mentioned such a prosaic thing. Preparations were begun. My mother made shortbread and cakes, orange and Madeira; she also gave two cockerels, plucked and ready for the oven, with a big bowl of stuffing which the Liddy girl could put in the birds at the last minute. She even put in a darning needle and green thread so that the rear ends of the chickens could be sewn up once the stuffing was added. The bath was scoured, the bathroom floor so waxed that the Liddy girl slipped on it and threatened to sue, but was pacified with the gift of a small packet of cigarettes. A fire was lit in the parlour for days ahead, so as to air it and give it a sense of being lived in. It was not certain if the actor and Ivan would spend the night, not clear from the rather terse bulletin that was sent, but, as Barry pointed out, he had three bedrooms, so that if they did decide to stay, there would be no snag. Naturally he would surrender his own bedroom to the actor and give Ivan the next best one and he could be in the box room.

Nobody else was invited, but that was to be expected, since after all it was a working occasion and Barry was going to pick their brains about the interpretation of the play, about the sets and the degree to which the characters should exaggerate their plights. The guests were seen emerging from a big old-fashioned car with coupé bonnet, the actor holding an umbrella and sporting a red carnation in his buttonhole. Ivan wore a raincoat and was a little portly, but they ran so quickly to the hall door that only a glimpse of them was caught. Barry had been standing inside the door since after Mass, so that the moment he heard the thud of the knocker, the door was swung open and he welcomed them into the cold but highly polished corridor. We know that they partook of lunch because the Liddy girl told how she roasted the birds to a T, added the potatoes for roasting at the correct time, and placed the lot on a warmed platter with carving knife and carving fork to one side. She had knocked on the parlour door to ask if Barry wanted the lunch brought in, but he had simply told her to leave it in the hatch and that he would get it himself, as they were in the thick of an intense discussion. She grieved at not being able to serve the lunch, because it meant both that she could not have a good look at the visitors and that she would not get a handsome tip.

It was about four o'clock in the afternoon when the disturbance happened. I had gone over there because of being possessed by a mad hope that they would do a reading of the play, and that I would be needed to play some role, even if it was a menial one. I stood in the doorway of the drapery shop across the street, visible if Barry should lift the net curtain and look out. Indeed, I believed he would and I waited quite happily. The village was quiet and sunk in its after-dinner somnolence, with only myself and a few dogs prowling about. It had begun to spatter with rain. I heard a window being raised and was stunned to see the visitors on the small upstairs balcony, dressed in outlandish women's clothing. I should have seen disaster then, except that I thought they were women, that other visitors, their wives perhaps, had come unbeknownst to us. When I saw Barry in a maroon dress, larking, I ducked down, guessing the awful truth. He was calling, 'Friends, Romans, countrymen.' Already three or four people had come to their doorways, and soon there was a small crowd looking up at the appalling spectacle of three drunk men pretending to be women. They were all wearing pancake makeup and were heavily rouged. The actor also wore a string of pearls and kept hitting the other two in jest. Ivan was wearing a pleated skirt and a low-cut white blouse, with falsies underneath. The actor had on some kind of toga and was shouting wild endearments and throwing kisses.

The inflamed owner of the drapery shop asked me how long these antics had been going on.

'I don't know,' I said, my face scarlet, every bit of me wishing to vanish. Yet I followed the crowd as they moved, inexorably, towards the balcony, all of them speechless, as if the spectacle had robbed them of their reason. It was in itself like a crusade, this fanatic throng moving towards assault.

Barry wore a tam-o'-shanter and looked uncannily like a girl. It gave me the shivers to see this metamorphosis. He even tossed his neck like a girl, and you would no longer believe he was bald. The actor warmed to the situation and started calling people 'ducky' and 'Cinders', while also reciting snatches from Shakespeare. He singled people out. So carried away was he by the allure of his performance that the brunette wig he was wearing began to slip, but determined to be a sport about this, he took it off, doffed it to the crowd and replaced it again. One of the women, a Mrs Gleeson, fainted, but more attention was being paid to the three performers than to her, so she had to stagger to her feet again. Seeing that the actor was stealing the scene, Ivan did something terrible: he opened the low-cut blouse, took out the falsies, tossed them down to the crowd and said to one of the young men, 'Where there's that, there's plenty more.' The young man in question did not know what to do, did not know whether to pick them up and throw them back or challenge the strangers to a fight. The actor and Ivan then began arguing and vied with each other as to who was the most fetching. Barry had receded and was in the doorway of the upper room, still drunk, but obviously not so drunk as to be indifferent to the calamity that had occurred.

The actor, it seemed, had also taken a liking to the young man whom Ivan had thrown the falsies to, and now holding a folded scroll, he leaned over the wrought iron, looked down directly at the man, brandished the scroll and said, 'It's bigger than that, darling.' At once the locals got the gist of the situation and called on him to come down so they could beat him to a pulp. Enthused now by their heckling, he stood on the wobbly parapet and began to scold them, telling them there were some naughty skeletons in their lives and that they couldn't fool him by all pretending to be happily married men. Then he said something awful: he said that the great Oscar Wilde had termed marriage bed 'the couch of lawful lust'. A young guard arrived and called up to the actor to please recognize that he was causing a disturbance to the peace as well as scandalizing innocent people.

'Come and get me, darling,' the actor said and wriggled his forefinger, like a saucy heroine in a play. Also, on account of being drunk he was swaying on this very rickety parapet.

'Come down now,' the guard said, trying to humour him a bit, because he did not want the villagers to have a death on their hands. The actor smiled at this note of conciliation and called the guard 'Lola', and asked if he ever used his big baton anywhere else, and so provoked the young guard and so horrified the townspeople that already men were taking off their jackets to prepare for a fight.

'Beat me, I love it,' he called down while they lavished dire threats on him. Ivan, it seemed, was now enjoying the scene and did not seem to mind that the actor was getting most of the attention and most of the abuse. Two ladders were fetched and the young guard climbed up to arrest the three men. The actor teased him as he approached. The doctor followed, vowing that he would give them an injection to silence their filthy tongues. Barry had already gone in, and Ivan was trying to mollify them, saying it was all clean fun, when the actor put his arms around the young guard and lathered him with frenzied kisses. Other men hurried up the ladder and pushed the culprits into the bedroom so that people would be spared any further display of lunacy. The French doors were closed, and shouting and arguments began. Then the voices ceased as the offenders were pulled from the bedroom to the room downstairs, so that they could be carted into the police van which was now waiting. People feared that maybe these theatrical villains were armed, while the women wondered aloud if Barry had had these costumes and falsies and things, or if the actors had brought them. It was true that they had come with two suitcases. The Liddy girl had been sent out in the rain to carry them in. The sergeant who now arrived on the scene called to the upper floor, but upon getting no answer went around to the back of the house, where he was followed by a straggle of people. The rest of us waited in front, some of the opinion that the actor was sure to come back onto the balcony, to take a bow. The smaller children went from the front to the back of the house and returned to say there had been a terrible crash of bottles and crockery. The dining-room table was overturned in the fracas. About ten minutes later they came out by the back door, each of the culprits held by two men. The actor was wearing his green suit, but his makeup had not been fully wiped off, so that he looked vivid and startled, like someone about to embark on a great role. Ivan was in his raincoat and threatening aloud to sue unless he was allowed to speak to his solicitor. He called the guards and the people 'rabble'. The woman who had fainted went up to Barry and vehemently cursed him, while one of the town girls had the audacity to ask the actor for his autograph. He shouted the name of the theatre in Dublin to which she could send for it. Some said that he would never again perform in that or any theatre, as his name was mud.

When I saw Barry waiting to be bundled into the van like a criminal, I wanted to run over to him, or else to shout at the locals, disown them in some way. But I was too afraid. He caught my eye for an instant. I don't know why it was me he looked at, except perhaps he was hoping he had a friend, he was hoping our forays into drama had made a bond between us. He looked so abject that I had to look away and instead concentrated my gaze on the shop window, where the weighing scales, the ham slicer and all the precious commodities were like props on an empty stage. From the side of my eye I saw him get into the big black van and saw it drive away with all the solemnity of a hearse.

LONG DISTANCE

AH, THE SNUG LITTLE HIDEAWAY with its cushions and its inscrutable Buddha, dim lights like scalloped stars in various niches and the gleam of the fire on the red-brown leather upholstery. So warm, so mischievous. Winter was almost upon them. Yet, the glow of the fire and that boyish smile on his newly shaven face, smiling the smile of infancy and boyhood and puberty and manhood, eating the nuts, the salt occasionally on his lips like a bit of frost which he licked as he would have licked her hands gladly. How long was it? He probably had forgotten. A party, a chance thing had brought them together again. Ah, that first time. Vertigo at the top of the staircase in a ponderous London club with portraits everywhere of gouty faces, faces bespeaking lust and disgust, and how they whispered though they were strangers. 'Swift as the lightning in the collied night,' she had said to him. Such a peculiar thing to say but he saw it as an anthem. Now he was telling her that he had learned a proverb, it was this: that the eyes are in the fingertips. He had learned it in the Far East: he often went. He worked all over the world designing hotels and airports and helicopter launches and he employed God knows how many, but he still had a boyish quality and was saying 'Is that dress new?' as if they had met just yesterday or at most last week. There wasn't a trace of bitterness in his voice or in his eyes, the grey eyes with the tenderest flinch. He had probably quite forgotten how it had ended, forgotten the late-night calls, the mad curses she had visited on him, the cold rodent glances he gave her when they met once at a summer party. He was conscious again, as if for the first time, of her radiance, this woman in a black dress, composed and at the same time reeking wildness. Of course much was concealed. There was behind that composed face of hers, with its high patch of blush, another being, in some ways more beautiful, in some ways more ugly and certainly more hungry, sucking him in, drawing him in, in, in, if only for the moment, if only for that hour while they were together. He would have whisked her away anywhere, given her anything; he was her slave through and through. What was he telling her? Yes, how he had learned to ski and how exhilarating it was, a new thing, and now he had two hobbies instead of one; his boats and the ski slopes. Oh yes, and he had named his boat after a saint. He did not say if she had crossed his mind in the intervening years but she must have, an image now and then, a thread of vexation about the bitter bilious letter she had sent to his home and was read, oh yes, read, and the nicer moment too, at a house party, at dusk in a grand house, all the ladies weighted with jewels, and catching sight of someone just like her with a flower in her hair, a bit of bougainvillea picked off a tree; or being alone in a strange city and looking out onto a harbour with its necklace of lights, lights glinting – so many eyes stuck into the mountain of night – and wishing she would appear by his side. Oh yes, he would have thought of her, not often but at those tenderest of moments when he forgot work and forgot ambition and put aside the little gnawing dream he had to run the world and listened to his truer self.

She, too, had of course remembered him but gradually stamped upon it, foot upon foot, grinding it zealously into any piece of earth or street she stood upon, burying it, burying him, clothes, shoes, braces, wallet and all. He had come in dreams, always retransported to her original terrain, always alone, on a wall or a headland or standing on a pathway under a tree, a priestly figure waiting to chastise her, not quite welcoming her but not dismissing her either.

'Did you ever dream of me?' she asked lightly, in a bantering way.

'All the time,' he said in the softest of voices. Now what did that mean? What was he saying? Were they good dreams, bad dreams, crowded dreams? In those dreams were they united or were they apart like those Japanese figures on a plate in which the lovers are perpetually divided by cruel waters? She also wanted to ask if, when he dreamt of her, he saw her in her happy guise, all aglow, or with a pulpy, tear-stained, supplicant face. It meant so much to her to know that little thing, the consistency of the image of her that roamed his mind. She didn't ask.

How had she spent the summer? In every question and every remark tossed back and forth between lovers who have not played out the last fugue, there is one question and it is this – 'Is there someone new?' The old entanglements, of course, remain like milestones and can be countenanced, but someone new can make an upheaval. That someone new might be the one to put a sledgehammer to those milestones, reduce them to rubble. She was telling about her holiday, the grandeur of it, a bay of course, yachts, canny people who talked always of hobbies and resorts, things they could share out in the open, never talking about the things they had in their vaults, their jewellery or their money or their savage secrets. She was describing it: her own little bungalow and a personal maid called Lupa who became so devoted to her that when she scrubbed the floors and made the bed and stacked it with a compilation of pillows and chenille, sausage-shaped cushions, she lingered. Then what did Lupa do next? She took to washing the faces of the flowers outside, washing each face as if it was a baby's face, first with a damp cloth and then with a less damp cloth and then a dry cloth, pulling off dead leaves as she went, putting them into a pile, and then going and getting a dustpan to shovel up the dead leaves, sweeping slowly, slowly, reluctant to go. What she did not tell him was that on one of those days, during one of those several sweepings, she had shed tears, many tears. They had simply gushed out of her in a huge flow, like a blood flow. Were they for him? Partly. But they were also for life, its heartlessness, and her qualms about losing something incarnate in herself. Lupa, who was hovering, saw these tears, crossed and stood in front of her, pulling down the lower lid of one of her own eyes to emphasize that she understood. Maybe she was saying that it was no joke to be a maid, irking to be fated to work for people who only spoke three or four words and these three or four words were 'Breakfast', 'Immediately', 'Iron', 'Wash', a maid whose wardrobe was not silk and satin but broom and mop made of cut-up rags. The moment had etched itself. There were three urns with plumbago flowers, water making fretful shadows on a bit of white wall, a lizard clinging to it, inanimate as a piece of jade. The maid was disappointed in her, yes, truly; tears were for the starving, not for ladies who had bowls of fruit to gorge from and a four-poster ornamented with porcupine quills.

He did not have to order the next drink. They came quietly, surreptitiously, the previous undrained glasses carried away. What a lovely time she was having, almost as enchanting as the first except that she was a little braver now, and a little warier, and much more assured and determined to tell him those light-hearted tales about her travels, about seeing men one night chase a butterfly because it was not lucky, stamp on it, and a drive home through lonely countryside with all the houses shuttered up, the jalousies closed to give the appearance of dolls' houses, the inmates asleep and the mountain itself girdled in white mist, like a presence it was, so that one thought of a Santa Claus roaming about. Then she found herself describing the beautiful painting, red and gold, the colours still seeming moist, seeming to seep though it was centuries old. It was of the Last Supper, the faces at the table grave, shrewd and austere, and not necessarily devout, and then a distance away – the supper table was outdoors – a woman with half-torn garb, also red, but muddied; a prostitute on the ground with a baby in her arms. Had someone thrown her out there, or had she come back to supplicate, or had she chosen that position for herself in order to debase herself in front of those grave, shrewd, austere faces? Or was it that at last she had given up because disease had struck her?

It was not what he and she were saying that mattered, it was what they were thinking. They were merely skimming the surface of the years, hiding all the urgent parts of themselves, she hiding the vengeances that indeed she had conceived because she had been jilted, and he believing that she had betrayed him with that bilious letter. She would insist that her betrayal was because of his betrayal and so on. Tit-for-tat. Maybe that was why she thought of that painting, that above any other, a woman cast aside by judicious men. Luckily he was not able to read her thoughts because he had begun to describe a hotel in Thailand, where he had recently stayed. He went on about the beauty, the harmony, the uncanny way in which people served without seeming servile.

'You can get anything . . . anything,' he said, conveying his own amazement.

'Even love?' she said, picking up the cue. He smiled. He had wanted to get her to that word and had achieved it so easily; so insouciantly had he steered her to it.

'Love . . . you have to bring yourself,' he said in a teasing way. It only took a minute – or was it five minutes – to tell her that he was going back there soon and he was going alone and nothing would please him more than to take her and to show her the city. For one who was not over-lyrical, he went on about the flowers, flowers in the trees, flowers in the drinks, and then the flower-coloured floating dresses that the women wore. The streets she could picture too, narrow and with little vehicles, little tuk-tuks that people travelled around in, and, of course, the vivid colours and the all-prevailing courtesy. Yes, it would be charming and she knew it. He would be at his best. They would meet there. He would meet her off the plane, he in a light suit, a different suit, and he would help her into a car, or maybe those little tut-tut machines, but probably a car, and point out things as they drove along, then take her to the hotel and up to a suite that was spacious and they would stand in that big room, timid, timid as flowers, virgin lovers, in that land of flowers, everything ordained. Every bit of her wanted to say yes. Her eyes said it and the eyes at the tip of her fingertips said it and the flesh at the back of her throat ached at the thought of these new sensations. It was a place she had always wanted to visit, as if self-discovery awaited her there. The women, she believed, had something to teach her, a vein of patience perhaps. It beckoned. She was weakening The image that floated into her head was a field of grass overwhelmed by wind, each blade veering in the same direction, powerless. He was taking out his diary. It was an invitation to take her own out because, after all, she was a busy woman too. His touch on her knee was like a little electric shock, but pleasant. If only they could go there and then. If only he stood up and carried her. Yet her answer was firm. She knew what she must say. The little beads of ecstasy in her throat were turning to tears, salt tears. It came back in a blinding guttural flash, the pain when he had left, the savagery of it, his deafness to her pleas, his refusal even at Christmas to answer a telephone call, his forgetting her address, the address at which he had called in daylight and in dark and had once flung clay up at her window; he had forgotten that address, simple as it was. How she hated these thoughts rearing up in her, but she had no control over them; they consumed her. It was not that she hated him; she did not hate him, but that old grudge, like a bit of flint in the ground, had come up to confront her. His eyes were so soft, his face so pale and gentle, his manner so suppliant that she longed to say yes, yes.

'It's not possible,' she said, but in a tone of voice so suggestive and so laden with innuendo that it really was saying 'There is another, whom I cannot leave.'

'Even if you tried?' he said, his eyes smarting now because he couldn't abide the merest rejection. Also, he was taken aback.

'Even if I tried, it wouldn't be possible,' she said, and a whole landscape of flowers and silk saris and tuk-tuk machines passed before her like dizzying images seen from a speeding train. He leaned over to the table beside them and took the plate of nuts and began to eat ravenously. She wanted to take his hand and tell him why. It would have saved everything. She put her hand on the sofa and at that moment he drew back his, his white fingers curling away from her like the tail of a white mouse receding into wainscoting. He had come with this gift, this offering, these days wrenched from his life and she had spat on it. He looked around as he always did when he became irate, and said they hadn't done a damn thing to the room in years, they hadn't even given it a lick of paint.

'Let's have another drink,' she said.

'You can have one,' he said as he rose, adding that he did not see why he should sit around and have her tell him why she did not want to go away with him. She must redeem it, she must. She jumped up and saw that he was cold now, disapproving like those disciples in the paintings.

'But you see why I can't go,' she said openly.

'No, I don't see,' he said, even more irritable.

'Because I would have to come back . . . *we* would have to come back,' she said, no longer afraid of her emotions, no longer raving about bays and bougainvillea, but reaching right down to the root of the love or the lingering love that was there, hauling him out of himself, shedding the lies and the little pretences, forsaking the wobbly balustrade that had been theirs.

'We're getting carried away again,' she said, and shook her head solemnly to make him understand. He felt it. His hand on hers, now so gentle, like condensation, a hand which she longed to hold on to forever, a keepsake. Never were they so near as at this moment of parting. But they were parting properly, decently, as they should have done years ago, and now she loved him in a way that she had not loved him before.

Outside the light was unsettling insofar as it was still bright, but all the street lights had come on. People in cars, people walking hand in hand, posters on the facings of cable boxes, torn faces, torn half-faces, the red glow of the traffic signals in the distance like heated moons, drivers with set jaws taking issue with God, a white-shirted waiter listlessly hailing a cab, and in the park now – because she had gone in there – the treetops all close together, snuggling, whispering, the hexagonals of light beneath them, haloed by both leaf and drizzle. There was a drizzle that pattered onto the leaves and onto her face, and the fallen leaves bristled like taffeta as she stepped over them.

'What now, what now?' she asked, and walked with pointless vigour, unable to exorcise the sight of him in his old tweed overcoat, moving away from her, somewhat downcast, somewhat melancholy, but not showing the full hurt. That overcoat must be ten or fifteen years old. She was touched by the thought that he had not bought another, something more plush. Only love makes one notice a thing like that, love, that bulwark between life and death. Love, she thought, is like nature but in reverse; first it fruits, then it flowers, then it seems to wither, then it goes deep, deep down into its burrow, where no one sees it, where it is lost from sight and ultimately people die with that secret buried inside their souls.

A LITTLE HOLIDAY

IT WAS A BIG ROOMY HOUSE, about three miles from the nearest village, and it had iron gates, a rutted avenue, a weathercock, and a dilapidated conservatory. For years I had been begging to go there, to spend a holiday with my uncle and his wife. I was nine years old and a holiday was not something I was familiar with, but I imagined that on holiday one underwent some glorious metamorphosis and came home wiser and more worldly. The thing was to be worldly, like the grownups. Going down the rutted avenue, in the front seat of the mail van, I admired the iron gates and the weathercock, but when the driver asked if I was going to spend the whole summer there my heart gave a little lurch.

Inside, the house was just as my sisters had boasted, but, then, they had gone together and I was alone. There were such relics of grandeur as a stately sideboard with a silver tea set and silver ladles, and a marble fireplace, which, alas, had chicken wire over it, to catch the crows' nests when they fell. Upstairs was worse. As I crossed the threshold of my bedroom, the flowered basin and ewer rattled in the metal holder, everything rattled and the wind keened like a banshee. The view of the blue-black lake through the window gave me the shudders, worsened by the fact that my aunt was saying I was a lucky girl to be put in the second-best room, with a view of the lake, a panoramic view.

'Where do you sleep?' I asked. The question was an affront to her whole status. She said they slept in the master bedroom. But where? Across the landing and down some steps. She pointed to it. She then showed me the bathroom – or rather, the WC. It was spotlessly clean, with a slab of pink scouring powder on a saucer on the floor, and in the yellow veined bowl of the lavatory was the name of the maker in blue dye. She said to remember to always wash after I had been to the WC, and not to ask impertinent questions. I knew that I would not be able to stay there and would soon be begging to go home. A bit of snivelling began.

'Don't be a mollycoddle,' she said. She brought me outside to get some fresh air into my lungs, as if we had not had fresh air at home – as if the whole country were not full of fresh air and mutinous winds.

There were very old trees on the grounds, groaning and swaying, their roots bulging like veins, and here and there were primroses that also seemed to fret. She left me in the side yard with a stationery box full of old photographs to amuse myself. Brown and sepia photographs, of her and my uncle, the house in its better days, when the conservatory had a roof, the various grandees who had come during the dapping season, when the mayfly was up. In those days she had kept a few paying guests, because there was not a hotel for thirty miles around. She used to glory in it and tell my mother that guests never tasted home cooking like hers. Roast lamb, roast suckling pig, apple crumble done in the pot oven with coals above and coals underneath to make it crisp, with the centre moist the way it should be, and the whole thing served with a butter sauce. Custard sauce was for people like my mother – ignoramuses. For those two weeks, during the dapping season, glory and levity had reigned. The gongs in the kitchen were ringing as the paying guests (they paid a pittance) rang for breakfast, or a jug of warm water to shave, or, in the case of one man, a large whiskey, which his wife begged him not to take. He had to have it, simply had to have it – for the shakes. Afterwards, when he had downed two or three, he sat in the deck chair and astonished everyone by doing the crosswords in record time. As a special, almost unheard-of favour, the mail-van driver would bring the papers very early in the morning so that the guests could read them and the drunk man could do the crosswords. I burst into tears when I saw my mother in one of these photographs, not alone but in a group, in which she seemed set apart – a misunderstood beauty in her box jacket with a very long slim skirt.

'Use your hanky,' my aunt said as she went by with a pan of mash. Eight or nine turkeys followed her, clucking. Soon my uncle returned from the village, carrying two rush baskets, his hat pulled down over his face. It was spotting rain. I could see he was angry; I could always tell when grownups were angry, either by their gait or the way they pulled their hats stolidly over their faces or the way they walked past and said 'Enjoying yourself, missy.' After he went inside I could hear shouting, and first he and then my aunt came through the back kitchen door threatening to leave while delivering a last volley of complaint and insult. Twice he came out with the baskets, and once flung one of them across the grass, dislodging bread, butter and tins of salmon. The tins of salmon made me hungry.

'In the name of Jaysus, can I do anything right, is everything I do wrong,' I heard him say as she gathered up the dispersed goods. I sang to myself, pretending not to hear – sang and hummed, staring at the photograph of my mother in the boxy jacket, which I knew to be of brownish velvet with ribs of cream in it. My uncle set off with a second basket and was going through the back yard, away from me, when she followed, crying and beseeching, begging him to come back, pulling him by the flap of his raincoat; his raincoat was quite stylish – off-white and rather like a motoring coat. Once they were inside the house, the quarrelling started up again as they each threatened the direst retribution. I did not know how I was going to endure it.

Hours passed. I could hear the silences followed by the sullen bursts of rage, and still she did not call me in. The dogs were fed, the hens and turkeys closed in for the night, and it was beginning to grow dark. I played with the red fringed tassel of the stationery box, and every few minutes had to pee behind one of the big trees; they were small dribbles such as puppies make in their litter, out of fear. The moon – or, rather, a bit of moon – came up over the boundary of the far field, and the lake water was so dark it no longer resembled a lake, because there was no way of seeing the surface, with its shivers. Corncrake and owl competed. I heard my name and rushed towards the back door. She fussed over me and said they had been so busy, said that not having children they were unaccustomed to looking at the clock and thinking tea-time or supper-time or whatever. They ate whenever they pleased.

'Isn't that right, Michael Patrick?' she said to my uncle, who was sitting by the fire on a cane chair, the front legs of it off the ground as he tipped backwards and asked if I was good at my lessons. She said I would be having supper alone, as it was way past my bedtime. I said, as forcibly as I could, that at home I went to bed when my mother and father and everyone else went and that I would not like to be banished upstairs alone. She said it was time for those bad habits to be corrected – time for improvement. She gave me a cup of lukewarm milk and some thick pieces of bread coated with chicken-and-ham paste. I refused to eat.

She said who would have supposed what a spoiled child I was. Hadn't I begged to come? Hadn't I written a letter? Hadn't I saved the money for the postage stamp? The milk tasted vile, as if it were milk from a cow who had just calved. She watched me bring my lips to the cup but decline to drink. She eventually lost her temper, poured the milk into an enamel pan and called in the dogs, who had been whimpering outside the back door but were exultant at this second repast. She said, 'All right, then, go hungry,' and laughed, but it was a hard, castigating laugh, and it was not lost on her husband, who winked at me.

My bedroom seemed miles away, farther even than it had seemed in daylight. It had an iron bed covered with two grey blankets and a white cotton coverlet. After she left me, I knelt and prayed. I thought that by violent praying God or the Virgin would do something to alleviate my plight. On the wall there were pictures of Our Lord, the Blessed Virgin, St Rita and St Joseph. The room was dark, but in the moonlight I could recognize these saints, as we had identical holy pictures at home, painted by an Italian who lived in the city and who depicted the sufferings very vividly. I needed to go to the WC, but I was too afraid to leave the room and make the journey down the landing in the dark. At least in the room I felt semi-safe because of all this praying and the saints watching down. She had seen me to bed with a candle but had taken it away, as it was the only one they had and they would need it at their bedtime. What to do.

Tears. Enough tears to fill the basin and ewer. Enough tears to fill the room. A lake of tears to fill the room. A lake of tears, an indoor lake. I eventually resorted to the unseemly strategy of howling, and as I howled the dogs took up the cue and howled from the outside. The whole place was a cacophony of howling where neither owl nor corncrake stood a chance. When my uncle and his wife came up I was on the floor, imploring to go home or to go to a hospital. At first, my uncle tried to pull me up, to put sense into me, but my hysteria triumphed, and she said there was nothing for it but for him to get on the bicycle to go to the village, to summon the Hackney car so that I could be brought home. He muttered that maybe the Hackney car was in Dublin or Limerick for some funeral, but I could see that he would go and that in some strange way the misadventure had cheered him, had taken the pall out of the night.

She helped me to take my clothes and things out of the drawer and put them back in the awful battered suitcase. She was sweet-tempered now, as she lamented the perils of being highly strung. She cited a cousin in our family: whenever she met people, especially good friends, her glands got the better of her and she simply cried buckets. I said I was very sorry for the trouble I was causing.

'No trouble, darling. No trouble, darling,' she said as she began to change into her good clothes. She changed in front of me. She had carried her clothes in from her room on a hanger. She was not letting me go home alone. She and my uncle would come, as they hadn't been anywhere since the ploughing match the previous autumn, and I needed coddling and escorting. A fresh fear engulfed me, which was that my own parents would be out rowing or would have gone to bed early, and that visitors would not be welcome. However, I was too frightened to mention it. She carried her shoes and her stockings in from the other room, and while donning them she asked me to redo the plait in her hair. Her hair was not as soft as my mother's; it was strong and springy, and she smelled of the talcum powder that she had showered over herself before dressing. Then she picked up the plait and wound it over her temples like a sturdy sausage.

In the car, she was a changed woman, all affability –

joking with her husband, saying she had once been a shy violet like me, hopeless in new surroundings, a misfit. She recalled how at twenty-three she had come home from America, back to her folks, and how on the second morning she resolved to leave again, unable to bear the rain and the pigs and the dirt and the misery of it all. It was, as she recalled, that very night that she went to the public house – not to drink but to see her old friend the owner – when she sighted her future husband playing cards with the lads.

'And we haven't spent a day apart since,' she said, to which my uncle lovingly agreed, both of them forgetting the times he went off on a batter, or the two times that she went to a home for her nerves, or the rows they engaged in daily and were known for throughout the parish. The talk was so lively that I now regretted going home, and then, to crown my ambivalence, she gave me a florin so beautifully warm and gleaming that I wished I were back in the bedroom, holding it, praying to the saints and at least waiting until morning to put them to this inconvenience.

At home, my mother accused me of being mental, whereupon my aunt intervened and said to feel my heartbeat and not to be cruel – obviously I was growing, and at 'that age', and full of unknown fears. My father came down with his trousers pulled up over his pyjamas and asked what all the commotion was. Upon being told, he said he knew it, he could have predicted it, youngsters were not reared the way he and his brother had been, and were not used to roughing it and being packed off anywhere, to any old relatives. My sisters were upstairs, asleep. The eats that my mother served were not very enticing, simply because, as she said, she had not been expecting anyone, and she wished it were next day, when she certainly would have made a cake, because she hated the house without a bit of fresh cake. My aunt said it was all delicious, although in fact it was stale scones that did not soften even after having been stuck in the oven for five minutes. My aunt told of a married couple who kept the top tier of their wedding cake for a christening, although they had been married fourteen years.

'I think they could put a knife to it,' my mother said sagely.

'You said it, ma'am,' my aunt said, and laughed. They never addressed each other by their Christian names, deeming it too familiar. My father and uncle were talking of the harvest, vying with each other as to who would have the best crop of oats. My father had put in three types of corn, wheat, oats, and barley, while my uncle had confined himself to barley and oats.

'In America they grow sweet corn. It grows on a stump, and they boil it and eat it,' I said to join in.

'Shut up,' my father said, and by way of sympathy my aunt touched the cuff of my navy jumper. I put the florin on the bread plate and played with it, both to let my parents see that I had been given it and to convey that I was willing to part with it, as indeed I was.

'That's too much altogether,' my mother said to my aunt. My aunt said she was sorry that she hadn't had the chance to make a pie for me or to bring me in a boat on the lake. They marvelled about the air and the beauty down by the lake. It was getting late. Soon they would go. The visit had no ripple to it. Part of me wanted to volunteer to go back with them, while another part admitted that that would be absurd. Either way, I knew that I had lost some part of my parents' love and God only knows how long it would take to win it back – days, weeks maybe, of slaving and washing up and shining at school. But even then it could come up at any time, this failure of mine, an added incentive for an outburst, another blind grope in which my mother and father were trying to tell each other how unhappy they were.

LANTERN SLIDES

'MACHUSLA, MACHUSLA, MACHUSLA MACREE ...' Someone would sing that refrain before the night was over; a voice slightly drunk, or maybe very drunk, would send those trenchant lines to all the boisterous hearts who, by midnight, would not be nearly so suave or so self-possessed. At first it did not seem like a song that would be sung there, because this was a smart gathering in a select part of the outskirts of Dublin – full, as Mr Conroy said, of nobs.

There were people from the world of politics, the world of theatre, the racing world, and the world of rock music. No rock stars were present, but a well-known manager of one group was there and, as Mr Conroy said, maybe one of his besequinned protégés would storm in later on. As Miss Lawless and Mr Conroy squeezed into the big hall, she saw a mêlée of people, well togged, waiters wading about with trays and bottles, and in the big limestone grate, a turf fire blazing. The surround was a bit lugubrious, like a grotto, but this impression was forgotten as the flames spread and swagged into brazen orange banners. In the sitting room, a further galaxy of people – all standing except for a few elderly ladies, who sat on a chintz-covered banquette in the middle of the room. Here, too, was a fire, and here the hum of voices that presaged an evening that would be lively, maybe even hectic. The waiters, mostly young men, moved like altar boys among the panting throngs, and so immense was the noise that people asked from time to time how this racket could be quelled, because quelled it would have to be when the moment came, when the summons for silence came.

Reflected in everything around her were the signs of prosperity – hunting scenes in big gilt frames, low tables crammed with ornaments, porcelain boxes, veined eggs and so forth – and the chandeliers seemed to be chattering, so dense and busy and clustered were the shining pendants of glass. The big flower arrangements were all identical – pink and red carnations, as if these were the only flowers to be found. Yet by looking through the window Miss Lawless could see that lilac was just beginning to sprout, and small white eggcups of blossom shivered on jet-black magnolia branches. It was a nippy evening.

Mr Conroy, as he led her through the throng, beamed. He was the one who pressed her to come, rang up and asked if he might bring her. They had walked earlier that morning on Dollymount Strand, had left their footprints on the sand that Miss Lawless had described as being white as saltpetre. On the walk they had relived several moments of their past. Mr Conroy had made her laugh and then almost reduced her to tears. She laughed as he described his love life, or, rather, his attempts at a love life – the coaxing and wooing of women, especially women who came up from the country and wanted a bit of an adventure. He spoke glowingly of racing women, who were always good sports. Then, in quieter tones, he talked of his first love, or, as he so gallantly put it, his first shared love, because, as he added, Miss Lawless was the other half of his heart's desire. Both Miss Lawless and a girl called Nicola had a claim on his heart, though neither of them ever knew it. Mr Conroy, who worked in a hotel, said it was amazing, unbelievable altogether, the things that happened in a hotel, the little twists of fate, and he went on to describe how one day, returning from a weekend off, he was told there was a lady drinking heavily in Room 68. He chastised the barman, said didn't he know they didn't approve of female guests drinking in their rooms alone. What he had to do then was ring the housekeeper and the two of them went up on the pretext that the room was going to be repapered shortly. Lo and behold, whom did he find but the sweetheart he had not laid eyes on for twenty years, who was now back in Dublin because her mother was dying, and who was, as he had to admit to Miss Lawless, blind drunk, her voice slurry and her face puffy.

'And what did you do?' Miss Lawless asked.

'I kissed her of course,' Mr Conroy said, and painted a picture of this girl as she once was, this vision who wore hats and veils and always put her hand out when she was introduced and repeated the person's name in a coquettish voice. Every man in Dublin had loved her, but she married a banker and emigrated to South Africa. She had come home only for her mother's funeral and, while she was there had died herself. At her own funeral all her former friends from the fashion world and the entertainment world convened, and, like Mr Conroy, they were desolated, bemoaning the untimely death of someone who had been so beautiful. Many made mention of her veils, and how she put an arm out when introduced to people and spoke in that unique voice, and all were shaken by the tragedy.

'We must commemorate her,' Mr Conroy had said, and all those gathered, moved by drink and grief, repeated his words and echoed his sentiments. It was decided that Mr Conroy would commission a bronze of Nicola to which they would all contribute. Alas, alas, when the bronze was delivered, months later, Mr Conroy indeed paid for it but did not receive the promised donations. It was, as he said, on his own mantelpiece, for himself alone.

But that was morning and it was night now – heady, breathless night – and Miss Lawless felt that something thrilling would happen to her. She did not feel like the peevish Miss Lawless who had put her stockings on in the hotel bedroom and given a little hiss as she saw a ladder starting from her big toe; and she did not feel like the Miss Lawless who feared that her black dress was a little too dressy because of a horseshoe-shaped diamanté buckle on one side, doing nothing in particular, just brazenly calling attention to itself. She saw now that her dress was perfect and, if anything, she was underdressed. The room was a pageant of fashion, and the combined perfume of the ladies, along with the aftershave of the men, drowned out the smell of carnations – that is, if they had any smell, because, as Miss Lawless reminded herself, shop flowers were not fragrant any more. Suddenly in her mind she saw old-fashioned climbing roses, their pink buds tight, compact, and herself getting on tiptoe to reach the branch in order to smell them, to devour them. This was followed by a flood of childhood evocations – a painted-cardboard doll's house with a little swivelled insert for a front door, which could be flicked open with a thumbnail; a biscuit barrel impregnated with the smell of ratafia essence, and a spoon with an enamelled picture of the Pope. Somehow the party had begun to trigger in her a host of things, memory upon memory, like hands placed on top of one another in a childhood game.

Meanwhile, coiffured and bejewelled, women looked around for the perfect spot in which to be seen, in which to appoint themselves, and their voices rose in a chorus of conjecture and alarm, repeating the selfsame remark: 'What is she going to do? I mean, is Betty going to faint?' Some were affirming that she would faint – those who were her dearest friends adding that they would faint with her, so excruciating was the suspense. They vied with each other as to this orgy of proposed fainting, and Miss Lawless saw bodies heaped on the sumptuous carpet, some in trouser suits with jangles of bracelets, others in ra-ra skirts, their gauze frills like the webbing of old-fashioned tea cosies, grazing their bare thighs, and still others in sedate, pleated costumes.

Mr Conroy was engaged in a bit of banter with two other men. Dr Fitz, a bachelor and long-standing friend of Betty's family, was assuring his two male companions that he had not put on weight because, like most modern men nowadays, he went to a gymnasium. Not only that, and he winked at Miss Lawless as he said this, but a good friend of his, a 'widda', had a Jacuzzi, and he availed himself of that whenever he dropped by.

'Oh, the floozy with the Jacuzzi,' Mr Conroy said, implying that he knew the widow. He then said that his weight never altered, simply because he never altered his diet, having a grapefruit and a slice of toast in the morning, a salad at lunch, and a collation in the evening. He was one of the few people in the room who did not imbibe. Mr Gogarty was younger than these two men, lived in London, but hopped back and forth, as he said, to recharge the batteries, and, of course, wouldn't have missed the party for anything, as Betty was an old friend of his. With a glint in his eye, Mr Gogarty brought it to the attention of the two other men that the city they lived in was a very dirty city indeed. They did not blanch, knowing this was a preamble to some joke.

'Haven't we Ballsbridge?' he said, waiting for the gleam on their faces. 'And haven't we Dollymount?' he said, with further relish, hesitant before throwing in Sandymount and Stillorgan. He went on to say that innocent people visited these haunts and never registered their bawdy associations.

'I believe there's a Carnal Way somewhere,' Dr Fitz said, not wanting to be lacking in a reply, and he pulled at the shirtsleeve of Bill the Barrow Boy, who stood nearby. Bill knew all these places from his early days selling oranges with his mother.

Bill the Barrow Boy was no longer a barrow boy, of course. He now mixed with 'the cream', being a successful broker. But he still knew his Dublin, especially the back streets, and was able to say that Carnal Way was somewhere near Wine Tavern Street, and that all those places were full of antiquity, so much so that if the pavings were dug up it would be proved that Ireland surpassed every other country in ancientness and memorabilia. He spoke with a Dublin accent, had a broad handsome face and a broad contented smile. While he talked he did a couple of card tricks, both to amuse himself and to prepare himself for the entertainments that were bound to take place later.

'Fourteen of us children,' he said to Miss Lawless, and boasted they were never hungry. He praised his mother – her thrift, her intelligence, her stamina – and described how she made money boxes out of cardboard, covered them with fancy paper, and how faithfully, every Saturday night, there were contributions to the coal box, the food box, the meat box, the candle box and the odds-and-ends box, in case any of them ever got sick.

'Made dinners for us out of samphire and cockles,' he said proudly. Although Mr Conroy liked to reminisce, he did not think that this was an occasion for recounting hardship, and, after praising the fortitude of mothers, he went on to draw attention to the gala that they were privileged to be party to.

'I was in on the secret from the first instant,' Dr Fitz said, stressing that he was a bosom friend of Betty's and of her children. Undeterred, Bill the Barrow Boy pointed to his bride, Denise, and deemed her the most photogenic girl in the room. He described their happy and healthy life, how they never drank indoors, except at Christmastime, and how they rose at six and played a few rounds of tennis before breakfast.

'Jaysus, it's like living in a monastery,' Dr Fitz said, and added that he had never heard of an Irish house that didn't have drink in it. Bill the Barrow Boy corrected him, said yes, they did have drink, oodles of it, but only for the benefit of visitors.

'Pardon my taking the liberty,' Bill the Barrow Boy said, lifting the heavy gold pendant of Miss Lawless's necklace. She told him it was Mexican but he insisted on believing that it had been dug up in an Irish field, as it was redolent of Malachy's colour of gold. Then he took her to task, in a joking way, for having become an exile.

'She's here,' 'She's here,' 'She's here,' voices said, and the urgent signal travelled back through the room. Lights were quenched, and those nearest the door kept calling back to those at the rear of the room to 'for Christ's sake, shut up'. Everyone waited, expecting to hear a little applause out in the hall, because it was those people that Betty would encounter first; in fact, the very first person Betty would encounter was the mime artist who had been hired for the occasion. There he was at the doorway, on this bright spring evening, wearing a black suit – pale as a gargoyle, moving nothing but one red-painted eyebrow, which he wriggled to amuse the arrivals. Yes, Betty would see him first, and no doubt she would guess that a birthday celebration had been arranged in her absence. She had gone innocently to the races and had intended to come home and have supper in bed, but her friends and family had foxed her and devised this surprise party.

'False alarm!' someone shouted, and the crowd laughed and resumed drinking as the lights were put on again and the waiters were summoned more urgently than ever, for people reckoned there would be many more false alarms before the birthday girl showed up.

When Betty did arrive, she took it totally in her stride, walked through the entryway, it seems winked at the waiters, and told one of the staff that the hall fire was smoking. Loud cheers hailed her as she came into the sitting room – a youngish-looking woman with short brown hair and sallow skin,wearing a coral suit and a coral necklace. She stood as an accomplished actress might, her hands reaching out to welcome a group that she certainly had not been expecting. She waited a moment before singling out any one person, but soon friends rushed to her, especially those women who had vowed that they would faint. People were kissing her, handing her presents, others were pulling her to be introduced to this one and that one, including Miss Lawless.

Mr Conroy said to Miss Lawless that it was a good thing they had taken that walk by Dollymount in the morning, or otherwise he would never have thought of inviting her. She agreed. Seeing her after several years – a little aged, but still glowing – it occurred to Mr Conroy that maybe there dwelt in some secret crevice of her heart a soft spot for him. He had seen her through love affairs. Once he had taken her to a fortune-teller on the north side of the city, saw her come out crying. Soon after, he had rung up a lover on her behalf, a married man, only to be told by the man's wife that he did not wish to come to the phone. He had had to report those uncompromising words to Miss Lawless. 'He does not wish to come to the phone,' he had to say, and then witnessed the hour or two of dementia that ensued. To others, she might seem composed, but he sensed that inside a storm raged and all those attachments battered her.

Suddenly there was a loud call for dinner from the chief waiter, followed by cheers and whistles from waiters and guests alike. All were relieved. A few grumbled jokingly and blamed Betty for having taken so long to arrive. Mr Gogarty asked where in heaven's name she could have been from the time the races ended until she got to her own house.

'Mum's the word,' Dr Fitz said, but the glint in his eye betrayed his indiscretion. He knew that she had met her husband and had gone with him as his wife to get the trophy that he had won.

The dining room was temptingly lit, and red garlands dipped from the ceiling in loops. The tables were covered with pink cloths and lit with pink candles, and all over the walls there were blown-up photos of Betty in a bathing suit and a choker. At the far end of the room there was a dais, where the orchestra already sat and was playing soft, muted music. Balloons floated in the air – blue, yellow and silver orbs, moving with infinite hesitation. Miss Lawless was seated with the group she had already talked to, and Mr Conroy introduced her to the remaining few whom she had not met. There were Mr and Mrs Vaughan, a girl called Sinead and Dot the Florist. There was also one empty place. Dot the Florist was wearing a pink catsuit, so tight-fitting that she seemed to be trussed. Mrs Vaughan – Eileen, who was in a grey angora suit – made not the slightest attempt to be sociable. Mr Conroy whispered to Miss Lawless that Mr and Mrs Vaughan had not spoken for over a year, but that nevertheless Mrs Vaughan insisted on escorting him everywhere.

'Any windfalls?' Mr Conroy called across, knowingly, to Mr Vaughan. It was their code word for asking if Mrs Vaughan had at all thawed. By his look, Mr Vaughan seemed to be saying that hostilities were dire. Sinead, who was in a black strapless dress, told her fellow guests, for no reason, that she was in mourning for her life.

'Cut out the histrionics, Sinead,' Dr Fitz said, and glowered at her. They were courting, but, as she was quick to tell the present company, he was full of moods. To his chagrin, Bill the Barrow Boy was not seated with his bride, Denise, a thing he could scarcely endure. He allowed himself a moment of misery as he thought of the one blot on their nuptial bliss. Denise did not want a child. Her figure mattered to her too much. 'Later on' was what she said. Many's the time he slipped into the Carmelite chapel off Grafton Street and gave an offering for a votive candle to be lit.

'Isn't Denise a picture?' he said to the others, and Mr Conroy seized the moment to remark on Miss Lawless's beauty, to say that it was a medieval kind of beauty, and that he believed that she was a throwback, like that queen, Maire Ruadh, who lived in a castle at Corcomroe, and who when she had her fill of a lover had him dumped over the casement into the sea.

'Didn't Yeats set "The Dreaming of the Bones" at Corcomroe?' Mr Gogarty said, with a certain bookish authority. Bill the Barrow Boy said he wouldn't know, as he never read a 'buke' in his life, he let Denise do all the reading, and assured them that she could read any ordinary book in a sitting.

'Oh, river and stream,' Mr Conroy said, as plates were placed briskly on the table. Some said it was trout, others said it was salmon. In fact, things became rather heated at one moment, as Dot the Florist insisted it was trout, said she had grown up on a river in Wicklow and that she knew one kind of fish from another, and Dr Fitz said that any fool could see it was salmon, its blush diminished by the subtle lighting. Miss Lawless put her fork in it, tasted it and said somewhat tentatively that yes, it was salmon in an aspic sauce. Dot the Florist pushed hers away and said she wasn't hungry and grabbed one of the waiters to ask for a vodka on the rocks. Dr Fitz said it was a crying shame to drink vodka when good table wines were being served, although, he added somewhat ruefully, not as good as they would be if the great man of the house were present. He boasted to Miss Lawless that they had often drunk two thousand pounds' worth of wine at an intimate dinner party in that very house.

'Now, now,' Sinead called to Dr Fitz, not wanting the missing – indeed the vagrant – husband to be given any mention. She was on Betty's side; Betty was her friend; she made it clear that Betty had poured her heart out to her often, and that she well knew the evenings Betty had supper alone on a tray in her bedroom, like many another jilted woman. Then, fearing that she might have betrayed a friendship, she commented on Betty's figure and, pointing to the various blown-up photos of Betty all over the room, she asked aloud, 'Why would any man leave a beautiful woman like that for a slut!' Why indeed? Dr Fitz told her to pipe down and not to talk about people she knew nothing about. Yet he was pleased to tell Miss Lawless in confidence one or two things about Betty's rival, a Danish woman called Clara. Miss Lawless somehow envisaged her as being blond with very long legs, and also as being very assured.

'Not a bit of it,' Dr Fitz said, and described a woman who was not at all svelte, who wore ordinary clothes, had never gone to a hairdresser or a beauty parlour in her life, and was overweight.

'So why did he run off with her?' Miss Lawless asked, genuinely mystified.

'She makes him feel good,' Dr Fitz said, and by the way he gulped a swig of wine he seemed to express a desire for such a woman and not the needful, tempestuous Sinead.

Mr Vaughan and Mr Conroy were in a pleasing exchange on the subject of Mr Conroy's tie. Nothing pleased Mr Conroy more than to relate yet again the story of how he came to get such a beautiful tie and what a double-edged gift it was. It had been given to him, he said, by a very generous lady, a rich lady whose baby he was godfather to. One day at the races, the tie was admired by a bloke and Mr Conroy heard himself saying rather gallantly, 'Oh, I'll get you one, Seamus,' thinking to himself that all he had to do was to go into Switzer's or Brown Thomas's and fork out fifteen quid and be in the good books of this man, Seamus, whom he had reason to want to befriend. Seamus used to do night work in Mr Conroy's hotel, but had been summarily dismissed because of incivility. Late at night, when guests from overseas arrived, he would tell them to 'feck off', as he was too lazy to get up from the stool and help with a suitcase or open a door. However, the fellow they got to replace him was even worse and an alcoholic, to boot, so they hoped to coax Seamus back. Lo and behold, as he confessed, the next day he scoured the shops, to find there was no tie like it, not even one approaching it. He finally had to ring the rich woman's secretary – the woman herself was always travelling – only to be told, 'Didn't you know? That's a very special tie. That's a Gucci tie.'

'Is that so?' he claims to have said, telling everyone at the table of his naïvety, but meaning it for Miss Lawless in particular. He added that one label was the same as another to him, and he knew a fellow in England, a foreman who worked on a building site, and he sent the tie over for a duplicate to be bought. After a couple of weeks, back it came with its companion in a regal box, and, Christ, wasn't it forty-eight pounds fifty pence. A shocker altogether, as everyone agreed, and the other men now began to stare at the tie with incomprehension. Sinead and Dot looked at each other quite piqued, and Sinead announced that the ladies would like a bit of stimulating conversation – they had not come to a party to be treated like ornaments, as was the case with most women in Ireland. She added that though they were treated like pieces of china at a party, they were frequently 'knocked about' at home.

'Bollocks,' Dr Fitz said, and by the way he picked up a bottle of wine it appeared he might brain Sinead with it. His cheeks were getting flushed and he proceeded to loosen his tie.

'So set us an agenda,' Mr Gogarty, the aggrieved divorcé, said, also nettled by Sinead's remark. For some unfortunate reason, divorce was pounced upon as a subject, so the table became even more heated, with men and women shouting each other down. The men insisted that divorce was wrong, because of the way children suffer, while the women claimed vociferously that children suffered anyhow, because their fathers were always in the boozer or in the backs of motorcars necking with younger women. Mrs Vaughan was the sole female voice who took issue with the other women, adding that young girls nowadays were tramps in the way they dressed and the way they behaved.

'How do you know how we behave?' Sinead said tartly.

'What's right is right,' Eileen Vaughan said, pushing her plate away contemptuously and applying herself to cutting bread into infinitesimal pieces, which she did not touch.

Much against the advice of Dr Fitz, Sinead began to tell how she, as a young girl not yet thirty-five, had been the victim of a modern Irish marriage, and it was 'the pits'. She recalled coming into her own building one evening and actually finding the chain drawn on her door, then ringing the bell but receiving no answer, having to go to the apartment below and ask a neighbour to shelter her for the night, ringing the telephone number but not receiving an answer, and a few days later learning that the person he had had in the room when he had put the chain on was a call girl. When she tackled him about it, he said that he needed comfort because she had gone out and he was not sure if she was coming back.

'It's bloody ridiculous the way women have to kowtow,' she said directly to Eileen Vaughan, who looked like a weasel ready to hiss. Dr Fitz began to fume fearing above all else that the next thing Sinead would treat them to was an account of her husband's suicide, of the amount of pills he took in that hotel in the North, and of Dr Fitz being called, because he happened to be there on a fishing holiday. Worse, she would treat them to the long rigmarole about her miscarriage and her husband beating her brutally. He was right. She was off on her favourite target. The four days in the labour ward, other women screaming and groaning, but to some avail, since they did not lose their babies. Then the bit about her husband coming to collect her, her imagining a treat – lunch out, maybe, or coffee and biscuits in that smart pub off Grafton Street – but instead their going out the sea road, her heartening at the thought of a walk along the strand, with the dunes on one side and the sea on the other, returning to the spot where they had courted, as an appeasement, a reward for all that she had been through. Hardly had they taken twenty paces along that littered seashore when he began to beat her up. Sinead became more hysterical as she described it, more dramatic – herself on the ground, her husband kicking her, first in silence, then his beginning to shout, to ask why had she lost the child, why had she been so bloody careless. His child – his, his. 'You're mad,' she recounted having said to him, and then told of standing up and feeling battered inside and out.

Bill the Barrow Boy leaned across the table and tried to stop her, but the other men turned from her in dismay and towards Dr Fitz, who was appraising the nose of a red wine that had just been brought in dome-shaped decanters. On the surface, the wine had a violet hue. The main course was also being served. It was duck with roast potatoes and apple sauce, which, as Mr Gogarty said, was far preferable to steak on a spring evening. The light had faded, and in the dining room, what with the balloons, the waving wings of yellow candle flame and the high-pitched voices, the atmosphere was fervid. Many were popping streamers from the little toy pistols that were on their side plates, and these coloured wisps of straw weaving and wandering from table to table, shoulder to shoulder, formed a web, uniting them in a carnival chain.

'Now, what is the difference between Northside girls and Southside girls?' Mr Gogarty asked with pride.

Answers were proffered, but in the end Mr Gogarty was pleased to tell them they were all dullards. 'Northside girls have real jewellery and fake orgasms,' he said, and laughed loudly while Eileen Vaughan repeatedly blessed herself and, as if it were a maggot, lifted the streamer that joined her to Mr Gogarty.

Mr Conroy, in order to bring harmony back to the proceedings, recounted the morning's walk that he and Miss Lawless had taken, gloated over what a sight it had been, what refreshment, the air so bracing, not a ruffle on the sea, the sand so white – or, as he said, white as saltpetre, to quote Miss Lawless.

Yes, Miss Lawless had asked him to take her there, but it was not so much to retrace her steps as to find them for the first time. Twenty-five years had gone by since that momentous occasion on the dunes. It was there she had surrendered herself to a man that she likened to Peter Abelard. He was tall and blond, with a stiff, almost wooden body – a sternness and yet a seducer's charm. The first time Miss Lawless had sighted him was in a newspaper office where she had gone to deliver a piece that she had written for a competition. Readers had been asked to describe a day by the sea. She could not remember precisely how she had described it then, but today, when she walked there with Mr Conroy, she saw patches of sea like diagonals of stained glass, the colours deepening as the water swerved from the shore to the Hill of Howth far beyond. Mr Conroy had said that if she waited a week or two more the rhododendrons would be in bloom over in Howth and they could go there for an excursion. She knew, just as Mr Conroy knew, that the red rhododendrons they conjured up were mostly in the mind – talismans, transfused with memory. On the walk, Mr Conroy often stopped in his tracks to draw breath, said he was getting on a bit and was easily winded, then pointed to his elastic stockings and spoke of varicose veins. But in telling the story to the guests at the table he spoke only of a glorious walk where they linked and strode together.

Yes, the traces of her and Abelard were there, because of course he had cropped up again in her mind. On the evening when she had first met him, when she took her little essay to the newspaper office, she had had a premonitory feeling that something was going to happen between them, just as this evening, sitting at that table, she felt that something was pending. She remembered clearly how Abelard had taken her essay, asked her where she worked, and how he diligently wrote down her address and her telephone number – as a formality, but from the way he smiled at her she knew that he had some personal interest. When her piece was featured in the paper as having placed first in the competition, the editor had got her name wrong, so the flush of her winning was a little dimmed. But Peter Abelard pursued her. They began to meet. She tasted her first gin and tonic and thought not much of it, but afterwards there was a floaty feeling inside her stomach, and then she took off her gloves and touched his hand and was not ashamed. One night they met far earlier than was usual for them, took a bus out to the sea, got off at Dollymount, walked over a bit of footbridge and then down a road and into the labyrinth and secrecy of the dunes, with the high swags of coarse grass and the sandy mounds serving as beds. It was there among those dunes that she gave herself to this Abelard. Although she knew she had, she could not remember it; it was like something experienced in a blur. It appalled her that she had in a sense detached herself at one of the more poignant and crucial moments in her whole life. Nor could she remember much of the hotel where they went later on, except that it was a dingy place near the railway station, and that the bathroom was out on the landing and, having no nightdress or dressing gown, she had to put Abelard's blazer on when she went out of the room. They were near and not near. He would embrace her but he did not want to know anything about her. She wanted dearly to tell him that this was the first time, although he must have known.

It was not long after that that he introduced her to his wife at some party, and his wife, maybe sensing that she was the type of girl her husband might like, or else feeling extremely lonely, invited her to come to their house for an evening, because her husband was going away to England on a job. She could remember clearly her visit to that house, and three children in ragged pyjamas refusing to go to bed. Then, later, her sitting downstairs in the big draughty kitchen with his wife, eating mashed potatoes and sausages and thinking what a lonely house it was, now the rowdiness had died down. They drank quite a lot of whiskey, and while they were drinking and talking about the mysticism of Gerard Manley Hopkins the telephone rang, and so great was the wife's excitement and alacrity that in jumping up from the table she turned her ankle and knocked over a lamp but still raced. She knew or hoped that the phone call would be from her husband, and indeed it was. She told him how their youngest son had bellowed his daddy's name all over the garden, bellowed for him to come home, and that at that very moment she and Miss Lawless were having a chin-wag. Miss Lawless had wanted to confess her wrong there and then to this woman, but she baulked. Instead, they continued to ramble and drink a bit, and later she kicked off her shoes and asked if by any chance she could sleep on the sofa. In the very early morning when she wakened, she saw the garden through the long uncurtained window, saw clothes on a line and a tree with tiny shrunken apples that looked as if they had some sort of disease, some blight.

The secret affair with her Abelard ended, and in a welter of choked emotion Miss Lawless had spent half a week's earnings – she worked in a shop and was paid very little – purchasing a book of poems for him, a secondhand book. So determined was she to be discreet, and so certain was she that the good God would reward her for her discretion and her sense of sacrifice, that she slipped a little greeting card not into the book itself but between the brown paper cover and the frittered binding of the book. She felt sure that he would remove that cover and find the greeting, that he would be touched and immediately restored to her. He would come to the shop where she worked, he would whisk her away, maybe even take her to a restaurant. The lines she had copied onto the card were from one of James Stephens's poems:

And we will talk until
Talk is a trouble, too,
Out on the side of the hill;
And nothing is left to do,

But an eye to look into an eye;
And a hand in a hand to slip;

And a sigh to answer a sigh;
And a lip to find out a lip!

As it happened, her Abelard did not find that note for many years, but when he did find it he wrote to tell her, saying also that he had lately been dreaming of her, and that in one dream he cherished they were at the races together, and he wished he had never wakened from it. She had not answered that letter. She did not know exactly what to say. She believed that someday she might bump into him and then the right words would come.

Today, as she and Mr Conroy walked along the strand, she had in fact asked him how her Abelard was, and was a little disappointed to hear that he was almost blind now, and that he walked with a stick. Unthinkable. Much as Miss Lawless wanted to see him, she did not at all like the idea of meeting a blind man with a stick. Mr Conroy, who knew that she had had this fling, kept suggesting that she phone him. 'Or I'll phone him for you,' he said.

She said she would think it over. In another part of her mind she actually just wanted to find the spot where she had lain, as if finding the spot would redeem the years.

'Dollymount is ideal for courting couples,' Mr Gogarty said, as if reading her thoughts, yet winking at Mr Conroy, thereby implying they both had caroused there.

'I declare to God,' said Mr Conroy, 'I was with a girl out there at about one in the morning not so long ago when a geezer tapped the window and asked me for the right time. The pair of us jumped out of our skins and I told the blasted Peeping Tom where to go.'

'End of a lovely ...' Mr Gogarty said, but did not finish the sentence, because of ladies being present. Eileen Vaughan suddenly exploded, thumped her husband, and said that never in her life had she been subjected to such smut.

'Ah, the Meat Baron,' Dr Fitz said, ignoring the tirade and pointing to a tall, bulky man who had come into the room. He was wearing a light suit and a very jazzy tie.

'Hawaiian,' Mr Gogarty said with a slight sneer, declaring how money betrays on a man's puss.

The Meat Baron looked around smiling, realizing that he was being alluded to. Dr Fitz told Miss Lawless that the man had a great brain – a brain that could be used for music or mathematics, could have succeeded at anything, but that it happened to be meat he got started on, because of going down to the knacker's yard as a young lad and buying hooves to make rosary beads with. Dr Fitz said that his admiration for self-made men was boundless; he said it showed real originality; he said that people who had inherited money were often scoundrels, drifters or drug addicts. Money, he attested, could either forge character or weaken it. He calculated that, now that the Meat Baron had arrived, and including the other various tycoons already present, there was easily billions of pounds' worth of money up for grabs in that room – enough money to support a Third World country. Bill the Barrow Boy leaned across and said that he would not want that kind of big money, that those people who had their own yachts and their own jets often came a cropper – went out in the morning in one of these yachts or one of these jets and by noon were in a Black Maria, stripped of every personal belonging even down to their Rolexes. The Meat Baron stopped for a moment, looked down at the uneaten duck on Dr Fitz's plate and said, 'She'll never fly over Loch Dan again,' and laughed. Dot the Florist pulled him by the sleeve, but he was already walking on and did not notice.

Dot had a plan of her own that night. She had vowed that before the night was over she would dance with one of the rich men, whichever one didn't have his wife with him. The bank was foreclosing on her. The little flower shop that she had opened a year before was still a treasure garden as far as she was concerned, but the novelty had gone and people went back to buying dull things like carnations and evergreen plants. Where else, she asked herself bitterly, would they find mallows and phlox and Canterbury bells; where else were birds' eggs and moss and miniature roses tucked into rush baskets; where else were the jugs of sweet peas like suspended butterflies? Where, but in her shop that was really half a shop? The other half was a newsagent's, and she could hear the ringing of their cash register all day long, while with her it was a question of people coming in and asking if she had any cheap flowers. It had been such a success in the beginning: she was written up, photographed in her little jalopy bedecked with boughs and branches, coming from the market. But now – that very afternoon, in fact – a cow of a woman had arrived in a jeep and bought half the shop, for next to nothing, asking if she could have a guarantee that these were not refrigerated flowers, that they would not wilt once she got them in her drawing room.

Dot eyed the Meat Baron; she had met him before, and felt that with enough vodka she could perhaps lure him. She would have to do it. Otherwise it was a 'For Rent' sign above the door, with the newsagent taking over the whole place. Galling. Galling. Some would say she was lucky to be there, that she was there only because of being a friend of Betty's daughter. But she believed she was still dishy and an asset at any party. A gypsy who had come to her shop had told her to make the most of her Mediterranean looks. When the time came for the ladies' choice, she would ask the Meat Baron up.

———

'Ah, the arms of Morpheus,' Mr Conroy said, nudging Miss Lawless as they both looked at Mr Vaughan, who had fallen fast asleep, his head on the table. Mr Conroy then began to whisper to Miss Lawless, describing Mr Vaughan's ghastly life. His wife hid packets of biscuits so that he could not find them; she put his dinner on a tray at six o'clock promptly each evening and left it there even if he was not home for days, so that the poor man had cold boiled potatoes and tough meat most of the time. Mr Vaughan, like many an Irishman, as Mr Conroy conceded, had an eye for the ladies and had met this beautiful lady – English, mark you – at Leopardstown races and assisted her, it seems, in stepping over a puddle. As a result, he repaired with her to the trainers' bar, and as a further result coaxed her to pay a visit in the fullness of time to a rural hotel in the South of Ireland. The English lady turned up with two suitcases, was given a suite, and later in the evening was visited by Mr Vaughan, who spent two nights with her, wining and dining her in the suite, having the occasional drive to the seaside with her to get a blow of air, and having cocktails galore and even the little farewell gift of a Waterford rose bowl from the hotel boutique. Mr Vaughan naturally told the manager to send the damages to him, as he would pay the bill at the end of the month, when his wages came through. Mr Vaughan was a dealer in motor-cars and was paid monthly. It was in his capacity as salesman that he had first met Betty – sold her a sports car. The manager, a religious man and a teetotaller, condoned the illicit weekend, chiefly on the grounds of Mr Vaughan's being married, as everyone knew, to a harridan.

'No problem,' the manager said, and passed on the instructions to the girl in Accounts, a snibby girl who at that time was planning to leave the place and go to England to work in a health spa. The time came and Miss Snib, having paid no attention to the instructions she was given, sent the bill for the wining, the dining, the suite and the Waterford bowl to the English lady – Miss Beale by name. Miss Beale, it seems, was indeed taken aback at receiving it, and doubly taken aback at the huge amount that had accrued. But being a person who prided herself on her dignity – she worked in the City for a company of financiers – she paid the bill, then put pen to paper and sent Mr Vaughan a letter that was nicely balanced between umbrage and desire. She expressed mild surprise that he should prove to be so lacking in gentlemanly courtesy, but, being a sport, as she reminded him he had often called her, she decided that the cost was trifling compared with the pleasure, and she went into some very accurate and fulsome details about his hairy body on the peach cushions of her flesh, and luxuriated on the tussle waged between these two bodies – their all-night combat, and, as she said, his little black thing getting its way in the end, and then morning, which brought them not fatigue but fresh vigour, fortified as they were by a gigantic breakfast. She was glad to have paid for such a romp, she teasingly said in a postscript; she would pay again for it.

'Mon Dieu!' Mr Conroy said and looked up at the ceiling, where shoals of balloons were on their happy circuit.

The letter did reach Mr Vaughan safely, and, once over his shock – having rung the bookkeeper at the hotel and made a complaint – and maybe feeling nostalgic for Miss Beale, he put the letter in his suit pocket and went on a bit of a binge. He was away for several days and nights, seeing friends up and down the country, and returned to his own house and his wife, Eileen, a sickly man who had to spend two days in bed, with porridge and cups of weak tea. Unfortunately, when Mr Vaughan rose to resume work he was in something of a dither, having express word from his boss in Dublin that unless he got moving and got his act together and sold at least one foreign motorcar down in the windy hills of the Shannon Estuary he would be drawing the dole by the following Monday week. Mr Vaughan dressed hurriedly and set off with the zealousness of a missioner, even on the way composing a short rhyme that would further the sales of the car. There was going to be a display of these cars in a week, and he knew how to get the public interested. The rhyme he invented was borrowed from 'The Lake Isle of Innisfree' and went:

> I will arise and go down to Kinsale,
> Agog in my brand new Ford Fiesta;
> I will eat fresh oysters there
> And in the afternoon have a siesta.

In his haste, Mr Vaughan forgot to remove various items from the pockets of his other suit, and he was hardly at the crossroads one mile from his house before his wife, Eileen, was reading a description of his prowess, which, after eighteen years, came as a shock to her. She lost no time. She had the letter copied on the new machine in the post office, making sure that she oversaw the copying herself, and soon after all of his friends, plus his family, including his sister the nun, plus Eileen's family, plus his employers, were party to the ill-fated *billet doux*.

Soon after, Mr Vaughan suffered his first heart attack, going down the steps of a hotel, where he had presided over a sales conference that had boosted his standing – principally, it was rumoured, because of his versifying.

While she was listening, Miss Lawless suffered a slight shock. Before her very eyes there appeared a modern-day Abelard. It was eerie. He was wearing a black dress suit and a cream shirt with frills that reached all the way down the front, like jonquils. The suit seemed to be not of serge or wool but of silk, and the sleeves were wide like the sleeves of a woman's kimono. He was blond, with fair skin and blue eyes. The blue was like that glass that has been rinsed again and again and for some reason emanates a private history, a sorrow. He was obviously a man of note, because various people waved, trying to induce him to come and sit at their table, but he just stood and smiled, determined not to be stuck anywhere he did not want to be. 'There's a place here,' Miss Lawless said, but under her breath. She was not usually so flagrant; in fact, she prided herself on her reserve. Betty ran and kissed him, and Miss Lawless experienced a flicker of jealousy as she watched this newcomer squeeze Betty's cheeks while they laughed over some little private joke they had. Miss Lawless thought that, as he strolled with Betty, he had something of the quality of a panther. She felt that his shoes, which she could not see, were made of suede, or else they were slippers, because he seemed to walk so softly, he padded through that room. Mr Conroy suddenly referred to him, called him Reggie, and said how he knew him for the pup he was – chasing young girls, his wife hardly cold in the grave. There had been a drowning accident the year before, and this husband was swanning about in Italian-style clothes, getting sympathy off ladies for his tragedy, leading a game life of it, flying to London twice a week, where, it was rumoured, he had a flat.

Dr Fitz looked up and was not at all pleased at the attention Betty was giving to this Reggie.

'Too much of a blush in that woman's cheek,' Dr Fitz said, as he looked after them, and then he turned to Miss Lawless to tell her about the day Betty's husband had left her and how he, he was the one to hold her hand. A party of them were just getting on the jet to go to Spain when the husband – John was his name – suddenly said to Betty, 'You go on ahead. I've decided it would be better if we lived apart.' Here Dr Fitz hesitated in order for Miss Lawless to take in the brutal significance of the remark, which indeed she did. He then painted a picture of Betty, the pretty and ever-cheerful wife who dressed always as her prominent husband liked her to dress, which was smartly; who rode to hounds at her husband's wish; who rarely complained if he failed to turn up at a theatre or a concert; who organized lunches, dinners, breakfasts for fifty or more at the last minute; and who even overcame her fear of skiing – all for his sake. Betty, suddenly a husbandless, stranded woman. Dr Fitz dilated further on the pity of it, the shock the poor woman got, and how she went berserk on the little plane en route, going mad up there in the filtered atmosphere, with the pilot wondering whether he should turn back or keep going, or what.

'If I'd had an injection with me,' Dr Fitz said, lamenting even now how he had set out that day without his doctor's bag – a thing he had never done since. He described again the plane soaring through the cloudless upper atmosphere, having to undo the buttons of her blouse, having to undo her shoes, holding her down, telling her that the whole thing was a bad dream from which she would one day awaken.

'You two are like a pair at confession,' Sinead called across the table rather sneeringly. Dr Fitz went on talking to Miss Lawless, ignoring the gibe. Sinead, who hoped to marry Dr Fitz, had thought for a few weeks now that she was pregnant, and knew that if she were she would keep it a secret until it was no longer possible to abort. She would then use every trump card of sentiment and religion to make him ashamed of even the word 'abortion'. She believed she was doing good by keeping this pregnancy a secret. Marriage would steady him. He still had the schoolboy notion of winning over every new female, which he was now trying to do with Miss Lawless, for which Sinead could happily wring her white neck with its collar of gold. Yes, a baby would settle him, preferably a boy.

Miss Lawless did not look back after Abelard and Betty to see where he was being seated, as that would have been too noticeable. The fact that this stranger was in the room was enough for her and made her think, with a wan smile, how slender, how delicate, people's dreams are. Suddenly her lips, her fingers, the follicles of her hair began to tingle, and she knew that if she looked into her little tortoiseshell mirror the pupils of her eyes would be dark and glistening. That was how it always was when she admired someone, and she had not seen anyone she admired for a long time. Her excitement was utter.

'Your eyes are like rhinestones,' Mr Conroy said to her, but he believed it was the general gaiety that made her look like that. As for himself, he was thinking that, with the help of God, he would take her home, and on the way he would suggest that they have another sea breeze; out there, with the dark sea, the misty emptiness, and the Hill of Howth, with its rhododendrons about to burgeon, who knew? He did not think she would go the whole hog, but he felt she would yield to a kiss, and to kiss Miss Lawless was a lifelong dream. Miss Lawless and Nicola had caused him many a sleepless night. He had a pinup of each of them in his mind, constantly, these opposite girls – Nicola so dazzling, with her veils and her husky voice; Nicola so sophisticated, and Miss Lawless so shy and so awkward, with that big crop of hair and a bosom that swelled under her shabby clothes, the man's dress scarf with the fringing, which she wore for glamour, and her always spouting snatches of poetry to layabouts and drunkards who had only the one interest in her. To kiss her would be the realization of a dream and, as he thought, maybe a disappointment at that. He well knew that emotions often blur pleasure, especially for a man. He had been married, but had buried his wife some years before. It had not been a happy marriage, and he often thought that an excess of emotions was at the root of it. 'Too much love,' he often said to those who sympathized with him on the untimely death.

Sinead, now quite tipsy, was becoming even more miffed with the Doctor for the way he concentrated so utterly on Miss Lawless, and so she piped up and asked him if he loved her.

'Never say soft things to a woman or it will be thrown back at you,' Dr Fitz shouted. Young Mr Gogarty had to agree. Mr Gogarty had his own reason to be disenchanted with the opposite sex. There he was, a divorced man, quite well off, taking women to the theatre, giving them *pâté de foie gras* picnics on luxury trains, taking them to Glyndebourne to hear opera, and all he got when he brought them home to their front doors at midnight was a peck.

'Jesus, there's the queer one,' Dot the Florist said, and they all looked up and saw standing in the doorway a strange creature who looked around, gaped, appearing to be deaf, blind and listless. The newcomer had cropped hair and was wearing a miniskirt and a big woollen sweater. It was clear she had just come through the open front door, and Mr Gogarty remarked that it was shocking altogether that no member of the staff had impeded her. All eyes were on this strange girl, some even supposing that maybe she was invited as part of the entertainment. Miss Lawless felt pity for her. There was something so trusting about her, so simple, as she looked around with her big grey sheeplike eyes, mesmerized by the crowd and the balloons and the orchestra and, now, the huge bowls of pink confection that waitresses were carrying about, along with plates of sugared biscuits that were shaped like thumbs and caramelized at the edges. Why not give her one, Miss Lawless thought.

'It's a damn shame,' Dr Fitz said and castigated those outside who had let her in, because in his opinion she had put a kind of shadow on the room, as if she augured some trouble. Mr Conroy said they shouldn't worry unduly, because although the girl looked a bit odd she was no trouble at all; she often called at his hotel for a gaze, especially when any notables came to stay and the red carpet was out. She walked the city all day and half the night, but never begged and never said a brazen thing. He went on to say it was a tragedy, really, because the girl had come from a good family, and that her aunt had been a certain Madame Georgette, who made corsets and had a shop in Dame Street. It seems that the girl had been orphaned and the Sisters of Charity had taken her in, but that her particular quirk was to keep walking, always walking, as if looking for something. This sent a shiver through Miss Lawless. The strange girl stared into the room intensely and then made as if to move forward to join the party. A waiter stopped her. He was joined by two waitresses, who spoke to her quietly. Then the waiter reached up and took down a big silver kidney-shaped balloon and handed it to her, and she clutched it in her arms as if it were a baby as she moved off.

Once again Dr Fitz asked them to consider the pluck and individuality of Betty. He said that nobody would believe it, but that he could assure them, that that very afternoon Betty had stood beside her errant husband after his horse won and had accepted the trophy with him. He then leaned across and said that he could tell them something that would shake them. She had not only accepted the trophy with her husband but she had gone to the champagne bar with him to have a drink.

'You're not serious,' Mr Conroy said.

'God strike me dead, I saw them,' Dr Fitz said, whereupon Sinead tackled him, said she had not known he had been to the races and asked him in an inflamed manner to account for himself. Then it was why hadn't he taken her, why had he lied, why had he pretended to be doing his hospital rounds when in fact he was drinking and gallivanting. 'I'm not putting up with this,' she said, her voice cracking.

'No one's asking you to,' he said, but by his expression he was saying much else, such as do not humiliate me in front of these people and do not make a fool of yourself.

She was asking loudly if it was with Betty he went to the races, and now it was dawning on her that maybe Betty's friendship with her was also to be questioned, was another part of the grand deceit. Suddenly, unable to contain herself, she rooted in her crocodile handbag and flourished the first love letter that he had ever written to her. It was on ruled paper and had been folded over many times. The colour in his face was beetroot as he reached across and tried to grab the letter from her. They grappled for it, Sinead grasping the greater part of it as she rose and ran through the room crying.

'Ah, it's the hors d'oeuvres that's had her,' Bill the Barrow Boy said, meaning the nerves. But he was the one to get up and follow her, because he pitied her on account of the story she had told them about losing that baby. He caught up with her at the doorway and dragged her back onto the dance floor, where people were already dancing. Betty waltzed with the Meat Baron, her head lolling on his shoulder, and Dot the Florist feared that, after all, the Meat Baron might not be the one, that she might have to look elsewhere. Dr Fitz, feeling that it was necessary to apologize somewhat to the people at the table, said that Sinead had a good heart, and that all the beggars in Grafton Street knew her and chased after her, but that she should never touch drink. To himself he was thinking that, yes, admittedly he had befriended her after her husband's death, and it was true that he had fallen for that soft swaying bottom of hers and the plait of black shiny hair that she sucked on, but it was also true that she had changed and had got possessive, and now, as far as he was concerned, it was two evenings a week in bed and no questions asked.

All this time, Eileen Vaughan kept looking around the table wondering if at any moment someone would throw a word to her. None of them liked her, she knew that. Hard, hard was what they thought she was. Yet the day her world fell apart, the day she lost her last ounce of faith in her husband, what had she done? She had drawn the curtains in her bedroom, the mauve curtains that she had sewn herself; she had lain on the floor and cried out to her Maker, cursing not the errant husband but herself for being the sour, hard fossil of a woman that she was, for never throwing him a word of kindness, and for not being able to express an endearment except through gruffness. She had prayed with all her heart and soul for a seizure to finish her off, but she just grew thinner and thinner, and tighter and tighter, like a bottle brush.

At that very moment, Miss Lawless was picked up from her chair and swept away from her own group. One of the ladies who had picked her up told her that she was taking her to another table to meet an eligible bachelor. In fact, it was this new Abelard. He did not turn to greet Miss Lawless when she sat down, but she saw immediately that she was right about his eyes – they were a washed blue and they conveyed both coldness and hurt. His voice was very low and when he did turn to address her his manner was detached.

'I suppose you know my whole history,' he said, a little crisply. Miss Lawless lied and said that she did not, but Dublin being Dublin, he disbelieved her but began anyway to tell her how he had lost his wife less than a year before, and while listening to the story and falling a little under his spell Miss Lawless was also wondering if he was not a cold fish indeed. Although there were shades of her first Abelard, he was a more ruthless man, and she could see that he would be at home in any gathering – had sufficient a smile and sufficient a tan and sufficient savoir faire to belong anywhere. He recounted, with a candidness that made her shudder, the terrible accident and the celebrated funeral that he himself had arranged. It had happened over a year ago. It was winter, and his wife, who was always restless, had decided to go riding. There had been a heavy storm, and the fields were flooded and many boughs had fallen from the trees, but as soon as the storm lifted she had decided on this journey. He had rung her from his office and she had told him that she was about to set out with her friend. She went and, as he said, never came back. Mystery and conjecture naturally clouded the incident but, he was telling Miss Lawless, as far as he was concerned she and her friend had decided to ford a stream that normally would be shallow but owing to the storm had swelled to the proportions of a sea; that the horses had baulked; that one of the riders, her companion, was thrown and his wife had jumped down to try and rescue her. In their heavy gear, both women had been carried away. The horses, meanwhile, crossed the stream and galloped hither and thither over watery fields into other parts of the county and were not traced until nightfall. He said that he knew about it before he was actually told; felt creepy while driving across the wooden bridge that led to his house, going into his house, and finding two of his children watching television with as yet no signs of emergency. Then darkness fell and the groom came into the hallway in a great state to say riderless horses had been seen. It was like a ghost story. He became animated as he described the funeral, the dignitaries that came, a song that a famous singer had composed and sang in the church, and then the fabulous party that he threw afterwards. As he was telling her this, Miss Lawless was thinking two opposite things. She thought about how grief sometimes makes people practical and frenetic arrangements keep them from losing their grip; but she also thought that he had dwelt unduly on the party, the dignitaries and the newly composed song. He told how he had not lost his composure – not once – and how at three in the morning he and a few close friends sat in the den and reminisced.

'Was she dark-haired?' Miss Lawless asked, unthinkingly.

'No. Fair, with freckles,' he said, summoning up a picture of a girl bright as a sunflower. He added that she liked the outdoors and was really a desert girl.

'And what do you feel about her now?' Miss Lawless asked.

'She was a good friend and a good lover,' he said quietly. It sent a chill through Miss Lawless, and yet his features were so fine, his manner so courteous and his eyes so sensitive that she found a way within herself to excuse him. Leaning very close to her, he said that he liked talking to her and that perhaps if she was staying on in Dublin, they might have a drink or a bite. That thrilled her. She believed his resemblance to the other Abelard to be significant and that, whatever happened between them, she would not be detached from it, she would not blot it out, she would hold it dear. She imagined going home with him and sitting in one of his rooms, which she deemed to be enormous, with grey, billowing curtains, like a gauze sea, and their talking quietly but ceaselessly. She wanted him to be human, to be marked by the tragic event. She wanted to peel off his mask – that is, if it was a mask. Now her imaginings were taking a liberty, and she thought that if they kissed, which they might, it would not be a treachery against his dead wife but somehow a remembrance of her, a consecration. She wanted to lie close to him and be aware of him dreaming. Foolish, really. It was the night – hectic, amorous, intoxicating night. She felt the better for it, felt better towards him, towards herself and all those people in the room. She was making her peace with the first Abelard now, because it was true that for these many years she had borne a grudge – angry with him for ignoring the significance of their affair, and with herself for allowing him to. What she thought now was not of the aftermath with that first Abelard, but of the excitement and freshness when it was beginning – the shy, breathless feeling they had each imparted when they met, realizing secretly that they were bewitched. She suddenly remembered little moments, such as having her hand in his overcoat pocket as they walked down a street, and looking up at the sky that was like navy nap, so soft and deep and dense was it.

Betty's was the first speech, and it was very witty and plucky. Betty said that being 'of a certain age' was not the worst time in a woman's life, and then she made some light references to previous parties when she was not nearly so spoiled. Taking the cue from Betty, Dr Fitz walked slowly to the dais and deliberated a bit before speaking. He said that while wanting to wish her well – indeed, wishing her well – he could not forget 'the terrible day' when he had been lucky enough to be by her side. Several voices tried to hush him, but he went on, insisting that it was all part of the tapestry of Betty's life, it proved Betty had guts, and that she could stand there tonight and knock the spots off all the other women in the room. People cheered, and Betty herself put two fingers between her teeth and let out a raunchy whistle. Another family friend recited a poem that he had written, which made several guests squirm. Miss Lawless felt uneasy, too. The speaker, however, seemed very proud of it and grew more and more emotional as he declaimed:

When I look down at the soil in our troubled land,
I see its forty shades of green
And say to myself, Why isn't our fourth green field
As green as the other three?

A few began to heckle and say it was songs they had come for and not drip stuff. Abelard left the table, but by a signal – indeed, a colluding wink – he indicated to Miss Lawless that he would be back. She assumed that he was going to phone someone and thought that possibly he was cancelling an arrangement. Even his absence from the table made her feel lonesome. He had that lit-up quality that gave off a glow even though his manner was cold. Mr Conroy, seeing her unattended, rushed across the room and asked her if she had had any advances from the playboy. Shaking her head, she asked in turn what the man's wife had been like. Mr Conroy described a thinnish woman who drank a bit, and who always seemed to be shivering at parties and having to borrow a jacket from one of the men. Meanwhile, the last verse of the poem was being heard and people were listening with some modicum of courtesy because they knew it was near the end.

But when I look up in to the vast azure sky
Irish politics and history recede from my mind,
And in their place the glory of the Creator
comes flooding through,
And the sky and the stars give a promise of eternity.

Though the people were still cheering and letting out catcalls, they were also surging onto the floor to make sure that dancing would now continue, and to satisfy them the music was hotting up – in fact, it was deafening. This did not deter Mr Conroy from telling his rival, who had returned, that he had known Miss Lawless for many years, that he had driven her to beauty spots all over Ireland, and had copied out for her the words of the ballads that were so dear to her heart. Then he embarked on a story about how, a few years before, he had taken her for tea to a renowned hotel in the west. He had gone in search of the proprietress, Tildy, whom he found in the basement, ironing pillowslips. He told her how he had a lady friend upstairs in the lounge and wondered if Tildy could spare a moment to come up and welcome her.

'Oh, Mr Conroy, I'd love to but I haven't a minute,' he reported the proprietress as saying, and added that he went away a bit crushed, but hadn't mentioned it to Miss Lawless; and that later Tildy came up, in a sparkling blue gown, her glasses on a gold cord, and how she looked at Miss Lawless and said in a sort of sarcastic voice, 'Who do we have here, who is it?' Miss Lawless could see that Abelard had no interest in the story but was polite enough to suffer it. She felt that each of them intended to take her home, and she wished that it would be Abelard. Yet she could not refuse Mr Conroy; she had been invited by him. She hoped for some confusion, so that the threesome would be interrupted and Abelard might at least whisper something to her, alone.

At that moment, the lights were quenched and the guests treated to a fresh surprise. Miniature trees with tiny lights as thin as buds dropped from the ceiling, so that the room took on the wonder of a forest. The tiny evergreens suggested sleigh rides, the air fresh and piercing with the fall of snow. Then four waiters ceremoniously carried in a gigantic cake. It was iced in pink and decorated with angels, and crenulations surrounding Betty's name. They placed it in the centre of the room and Betty was led across to cut it, while two eager photographers rushed to capture the moment. The great clock in the hall outside struck midnight, but the pauses between the chimes seemed unnaturally long. Then a dog barked outside – a whole series of yelps, growing fiercer and fiercer, reaching a frothing crescendo, and then suddenly stopping as if overwhelmed. This dog, Tara, had never been known to be silenced by any but its master. Were a stranger now entering, the dog, even on its fetters, would be ungovernable. It must be its master. Who else could it be? Such were the words that people spoke, whether by a look or by expressing them directly.

'It would be awfully inconvenient now if it was John,' Betty said very loudly, the knife still poised in the big cake, the icing beginning to shed from the impact of the blade. And yet everyone hoped that it was John, the wandering Odysseus returned home in search of his Penelope. You could feel the longing in the room, you could touch it – a hundred lantern slides ran thorugh their minds; their longing united them, each rendered innocent by this moment of supreme suspense. It seemed that if the wishes of one were granted, then the wishes of others would be fulfilled in rapid succession.

It was like a spell. Miss Lawless felt it, too – felt prey to a surge of happiness, with Abelard watching her with his lowered eyes, his long fawn eyelashes soft and sleek as a camel's. It was as if life were just beginning – tender, spectacular, all-embracing life – and she, like everyone, were jumping up to catch it. Catch it.